THE DEPTFORD GIRLS

COURAGE, FRIENDSHIP AND BETRAYAL IN WORLD WAR TWO

PATRICIA A MCBRIDE

CORNFLOWER PUBLISHING

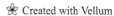

CHAPTER 1

'o, David Niven's best. Such a gentleman and so attractive!'

'Rubbish, give me James Stewart any day. He's my ideal husband!'

'Girls! Girls!' Mr Lynch said, his cheeks turning pink, 'we've too much work to do to... I must insist...'

'What about Clark Gable? He's a looker for sure!'

'Girls! We must...'

'What about Laurence Olivier? He's a proper gent!'

I'd just walked into the room, Bronwyn behind me, and was met with a ding-dong about film stars. As usual, Mr Lynch, our supervisor, was useless at taking control.

'Shut up, you lot!' I shouted, just as Bronwyn was saying, 'Kirk Douglas is so lush!' I looked at her and put my finger to my lips.

They turned to look at me, and the silence was deafening. Marion was fetching as usual with a bright red lipstick and eyebrows coloured with a burnt matchstick. She was a civilian working for the Depot. Edith, who liked James Stew-

---

CHAPTER 1

'No, David Niven's best. Such a gentleman and so attractive!'

'Rubbish, give me James Stewart any day. He's my ideal husband!'

'Girls! Girls!' Mr Lynch said, his cheeks turning pink, 'we've too much work to do to... I must insist...'

'What about Clark Gable? He's a looker for sure!'

'Girls! We must...'

'What about Laurence Olivier? He's a proper gent!'

I'd just walked into the room, Bronwyn behind me, and was met with a ding-dong about film stars. As usual, Mr Lynch, our supervisor, was useless at taking control.

'Shut up, you lot!' I shouted, just as Bronwyn was saying, 'Kirk Douglas is so lush!' I looked at her and put my finger to my lips.

They turned to look at me, and the silence was deafening. Marion was fetching as usual with a bright red lipstick and eyebrows coloured with a burnt matchstick. She was a civilian working for the Depot. Edith, who liked James Stew-

1

art, was in ATS uniform. Her husband Sidney was away at war and she longed for the day he came home.

I pulled Bronwyn towards me, 'Never mind film stars. I'd like you all to meet my friend Bronwyn, from Welsh Wales...'

'But I speaks English.' she said, interrupting me with her lovely Welsh accent.

'Bronwyn's my flat mate and she's been a dispatch rider til she broke her leg, and now she wants a sitting-down job,' I grinned, 'she's not so bad once you get to know her!'

They came round from their desks, shaking hands or hugging Bronwyn. Mr Lynch stood back until they'd finished.

'Mr McDonald warned me you were coming. I'm very glad to see you. We're snowed under with work. And tomorrow...' he paused for effect, 'we have another typist starting, Ruth Demsky. She's been at home bringing up a family for a long time, but is coming to help the war effort. She's a civilian.'

'Is this desk for me?' Bronwyn asked, pointing to one near me.

'There's only two to choose from and you're first here, so help yourself. Lily will show you round the offices and warehouse area, then I'll explain the work.'

It was a warm day for May, and Bronwyn and I were glad of an excuse to get outside. The sun was shining and cotton wool clouds scudded across the sky. By contrast, the warehouse area was uninviting. A huge triangular area, with three massive warehouses, it was bordered on one side by a railway line; a road on another; and the backs of terraced houses on the third. A tall fence hid the houses from sight, although it was there to deter people from pilfering the stock we kept. Weeds crept along the bottom like a fallen curtain.

To my surprise, there were two armed soldiers outside the

far warehouse. I'd never seen that before. 'Come on, Bron, let's see what they're up to.'

I went over to the soldiers and they immediately tensed - guns at the ready. 'Halt!' one of them cried, trying to be heard over the background noise.

'My name's Lily Baker and I work here. I often have to check stock in the warehouse. What's going on? I've never seen soldiers here before like this.'

'Better speak to your boss about it.' That was the most I got out of either of them.

Bronwyn looked at me, 'What's up, girl? You look bothered.'

I smiled, 'Nothing to worry about. I'll speak to Mr McDonald when we go back and find out what it's all about. Come on, I'll finish showing you around.'

A man with a very wide broom was sweeping between the lorries and buildings. He sang as he worked, although his words were lost because of the background noise. The air hung with the smell of petrol and the smoke from the trains.

'You bin looking at that warehouse?' the man sweeping asked, leaning on his broom, 'Strange that.'

'What's with all the security?' I asked.

'We're gonna be stocking guns and things is what I heard. Don't like the sound of it. I'd sooner stick to bully beef and boots meself.'

'So that's it,' I said as we walked away, 'guns. Blimey! Still, I suppose we are an Army Depot, so it's not surprising.'

I took her to another of the warehouses. Organised rows of shelves stocked with big, labelled boxes were against the walls and in the middle. 'See that little hut thing in the corner up the stairs?' I said, pointing, 'that's their office. One for each warehouse. Go there if you need to check anything, although usually you'll find the warehouse supervisor down here working.'

Lorries arrived, laden with goods, and then left again. Sometimes they loaded up with stock from the warehouses and took them to army camps, other times they went back empty to their factories to collect another load. There was a lot of clattering and banging and men shouting instructions to each other.

'I gotta say, I'm going to be spoilt for choice of men here,' Bronwyn said as someone wolf-whistled at us.

I raised an eyebrow, 'You like men with money to spend. You won't find that here; they don't get paid enough.'

'Pity,' she looked around, 'so will I have to come out here often then?'

'Sometimes you might need to check the figures you're typing to see if there's been an error. Mostly you'll be in the office. Come on, I'll show you around inside.'

We were almost at the door when the big boss, Mr McDonald, came out with a man I hadn't seen before. He was tall, well built, and glossy enough to be a film star. Unlike most people who came to the yard, he was wearing a suit and tie and his shoes were so shiny he could have used them for mirrors. He looked like he'd have enough money for Bronwyn to be interested in him.

'Ah, Lily,' Mr McDonald said, 'and Bronwyn our new girl, I'm glad I caught you. I've been showing Mr Biggerstaff around. He's already supplying some of our goods, but he's adding different things now.' His eyes slid to the guarded warehouse, so I guessed this Mr Biggerstaff was supplying arms. 'You'll be seeing his new dockets go through soon.'

Mr Biggerstaff stepped forward and kissed us on both cheeks. Having lived in Paris as telephonists with the British Expeditionary Force, we were used to that, but it felt strange in Deptford. There was something about him that made me want to shiver. It was hard to put my finger on what it was; probably he was simply too smooth. Definitely creepy. That's what I thought, but then I glanced at Bronwyn and saw she was interested. I looked at her and rolled my eyes; she poked out her tongue in response. I decided there and then I'd have a talk with her when we got home about mixing work and pleasure. Not that she'd take any notice of me; she never had before.

We were about to walk on when Mr McDonald spoke again, 'You can trust Lily,' he said to Mr Biggerstaff, 'she's a sharp one. A while ago she uncovered someone who was...shall we say... not acting in the Depot's best interest.'

Mr Biggerstaff's eyes narrowed as he looked at me again, 'I'll have to watch myself then,' he said with a smile that didn't reach those eyes, 'I'm John, by the way, no need to be formal. I hope we'll get to know each other better.'

Bronwyn and I said goodbye and went into the main office. 'He's lush,' she said, 'just my type. We never had any like him in Swansea. Bit old for me, he must be in his forties, but I could live with that.'

I shuddered, 'I hope you're not serious; there's something odd about that man.'

The corners of her mouth turned down. 'You're probably right. I'm turning over a new leaf. No more married men. Mind you, I'm still hoping to find a rich single one.'

We spent the rest of the time introducing Bronwyn to people and showing her where everything was. We soon forgot Mr Biggerstaff.

If only it had stayed that way.

B ack in our office, Edith was hurriedly putting all her things in her bag. She was rushing so much she was almost tripping over her own feet.

'What's up, Edith?' I asked.

'It's Sidney,' she said, sounding breathless, 'they just phoned here to say he's coming home this afternoon.'

'Is that your husband?' Bronwyn asked, 'he's lucky if he got leave.'

Hands shaking, Edith fumbled as she covered her type-writer and put her pencils away. 'It's not leave. He's been in hospital in France. No-one told me. He's got some sort of head injury.' She got out her hanky and blew her nose. 'I've got to go now,' she picked up her things and dashed out of the door.

'Well, there's a turn up for the books,' Bronwyn said, 'poor thing, but it means I'm needed more than ever.'

Marion looked worried, 'We do need you Bronwyn - but poor Edith. She's been looking forward to Sidney coming home for so long and now she doesn't know what's happened to him or what she'll be faced with. I hope he's going to be okay.'

'Lots of chaps came back from the Great War with head injuries. Turned them very funny, some of them,' Bronwyn said.

'Indeed,' Mr Lynch said. He looked at his watch, 'Why don't we have our break now, then we can really get cracking when we get back.'

CHAPTER 2

*E*xhausted from another night trying to sleep in the tube station, Bronwyn and I headed towards the bus stop early next morning.

HOUSE OF COMMONS BOMBED

The headline on the hoarding stopped us short. I fished some pennies out of my purse and bought the paper. We stood at the bus stop, wondering if the bus would come. So many roads had been bombed, buses were often very late if they came at all. While we waited, I opened the newspaper and read the article, 'It's not the whole of the House of Commons, only the Chamber that's been bombed, whatever that is.'

'They won't have trouble being rehoused,' Bronwyn said, her tone bitter. We'd been bombed out twice and lost everything both times. The same story was true for hundreds, thousands of people.

I read some more. 'It doesn't say anything about Churchill. I suppose he's safe and sound in his War Rooms in Whitehall.'

'Not being funny nor nothing, but I bet his underground

place is a lot more comfortable than sleeping in the tube station.'

'Can't blame him. We'd do the same.'

The bus journey took ages as usual; a different route each time. We had plenty of time to look at the latest bomb damage. A milkman, his white cap crooked, was walking over a flattened house, carefully carrying the crate of milk. The weight made him lean to one side as he balanced on the rubble. Then we passed the most incredible sight: a bombed library. It had no roof and wooden beams leaned from ceiling to floor, but amazingly, the walls were still upright, complete with books - intact. Two men were studying them as if it was nothing unusual, although they were standing on piles of debris. They gingerly walked over the debris as they looked at different books.

Bronwyn bent over me to look, 'Hope they're going to check those books out!' she joked.

In the office we settled down to our routine work, but worried about Edith who hadn't come in.

'I told her to take a couple of days off what with her hubby coming back,' Mr Lynch said, 'nothing to worry about. I hope they're having a good time after him being away so long.'

Our new typist, Ruth, arrived hot and flustered twenty minutes late, 'Sorry, sorry,' she said, 'the bus didn't come.'

She was short, not much more than five feet tall and a bit stout. Dressed all in dark clothes, she wore horn rimmed circular glasses that made her look like a professor. I could imagine her sitting at home knitting and chatting to family. Or standing in front of a lecture hall full of students busily taking notes.

Mr Lynch asked me to show Ruth around as I had the day before with Bronwyn.

'This is so kind of you,' she said as we headed for the outdoor area, 'I'm sorry to take up all your time.'

'Nothing to apologise for. I'm grateful for a chance to get away from the typewriter.'

We headed towards the front door, 'Most of the time you'll be in the office, but occasionally if you see an order is wrong you'll need to come out and see what's what.'

'Do you mean if they're on the fiddle? Am I supposed to challenge the men if I think they're dishonest? Look at me, I'm a little lady, not made for a fight. Sorry.'

I had to laugh at the image she conjured up, 'No, if you suspect that, you say nothing, but go to tell Mr Lynch. He'll speak to Mr McDonald, the big boss, if necessary.'

She patted her chest, 'Oy vey, that's good to know. There's enough trouble in life without that sort of thing.'

By now we were walking towards the first warehouse, 'What trouble have you had?'

'My children, all three of them, were evacuated yesterday. It nearly broke my heart saying goodbye to them. What if the family they go to are unkind? What if they don't get my letters? What if they don't write back?' She opened her handbag and took out a photo of the children. It was well worn from being handled so much. 'See, they're lovely children. So clever, so beautiful. I shouldn't boast, but it's true. She pointed to each of them. That's Aaron, my eldest, he's eleven and a big boy, full of mischief. Looks older than he is. Miriam is seven, she's very serious and sensible, and then little Judith. Look at her cute face, she's five and never stops talking. They take after my side of the family.'

I looked at the photo and thought they didn't look much like her but didn't say so. Instead I said how wonderful they looked. She carefully put the photo back in her bag, 'What if they don't love me when they come home?' she rubbed her fist against her chest, and wiped a tear from her eyes.

I put my arm through hers, and noticed she smelled of Lily of the Valley perfume. 'And what if it all goes smoothly? Sounds to me like you're one of life's worriers.'

She took a hanky out of her pocket and blew her nose, 'It's true, it's true. My family say I invent things to worry about. But what about you, my dear, how are things in your life?'

All went well until we went into the third warehouse. We greeted the men who were busy at work and went round so I could show her the goods stored there. Suddenly, she stopped and I almost tripped over her.

'Look!' she said, pointing to a wooden post in one corner. The post was covered in notices and pin-ups. 'I do wish they wouldn't put these pin-up everywhere. They're embarrassing. Those ladies with not enough clothes on, it's a wonder they don't catch a cold.' She lifted the picture as she spoke, then gasped and stiffened. Underneath was a small drawing of a Swastika. Her hand went to her heart again, 'Who would do such a thing? That means someone in here hates us Jews. We don't need more people who hate us, there are enough in this world,' she turned to me, eyes blazing, 'do you know who it is? I will tell Mr McDonald right away.' Her previous timid behaviour was gone; replaced by fierceness of purpose.

I had no idea and asked her to wait and see before she spoke to Mr McDonald. 'It might even have been someone who's left,' I said, 'I've never heard anyone say anything to make me suspect them.'

Her shoulders dropped and the tension in her face relaxed a little. 'Maybe you're right. I can jump to conclusions some-times. I'm very sensitive about it, even though I'm not a very strict Jew. Now, I was telling you about my brother-in-law...'

By the time I'd finished showing her round, I knew her

life story. She knew quite a lot of mine too. With her open attitude and warmth, she was easy to like and I looked forward to working with her.

When I had a chance, I went to see Mr McDonald. I'd got to know him well when I'd discovered who was fiddling the books a few months before. He'd always treated me as someone special ever since.

Despite this, I had butterflies in my tummy when I knocked on his door.

'Come in!' he called.

He smiled when he saw me. 'Sit down, Lily. What can I do for you?'

He pushed aside some papers and leaned forward.

I sat on the edge of the seat and twisted my hanky in my hands, 'I've just been showing the new girl, well lady, Ruth, around. It's probably nothing, but when we went to the warehouse nearest the railway lines someone had drawn a Swastika on one of the posts. It was covered with a pin-up, but it was there all right. Ruth is Jewish and she was very upset. So was I. Do you think we have a Nazi sympathiser working here?'

He sat back, his brow wrinkled, 'Did it look like a new drawing?'

'I'm not sure, it was hard to tell.'

He looked down and shook his head. 'This might be quite serious. The Depot isn't a major military secret, but we wouldn't want Nazi sympathisers knowing everything that goes on here,' he rubbed his chin with his knuckles, 'I think you'd better leave it with me, Lily. I'll go and look at it in a minute and decide what action to take. Thank you for telling me.'

I went back to the office and told Ruth I'd spoken to Mr McDonald about what she'd found. She was so pleased she leaped out of her seat and hugged me.

'I'm so grateful,' she said, 'and about work, my typing's a bit rusty, you know, but it'll get better. Please be kind and give me some leeway.' she said as she tore up her second piece of paper, 'I'll be extra careful. Mustn't waste paper.'

At the end of the day Mr Lynch stood up. 'How time flies; time to go home, girls.' And, as usual with him, he was out of the door before the rest of us had even tidied up our desks.

Ruth clapped her hands. 'Thank you all for being so wonderful to me today,' she said with a smile, 'I always have a special dinner on Friday nights. Would any of you like to come? It's kosher, of course, but I'm a good cook!'

I t was still daylight when Bronwyn and I set out for Ruth's place. 'We'd better get a bus,' Bronwyn said, 'we don't want to end up stuck between stations on the underground.' She looked up at the sky, 'Let's hope we don't have any bombing. You're very brave doing your Air Raid work after what happened to you when that bomb went off.'

I picked my way round a pile of bricks from a bombed house, 'I still have the scar on my forehead to remind me every time I look in the mirror. But there's talk that the Germans are turning their attention to Russia, so we may not get bombed so often. I hope not. After what I've seen I have nightmares almost every night. I keep seeing all those bodies, or bits of bodies, and crying mums and dads carrying their dead child in their arms.'

She put her arm through mine, 'I know you do, Cariad. I hear you groaning at night sometimes; you thrash about something rotten in your sleep. Sometimes I wonder if I should wake you up. Do you still dream about David? The man you cared about so much?'

I nodded, 'Often, but they're usually nice dreams. I'm glad I didn't actually see him die, or if I did I don't remember it. Head injuries do funny things to you.'

Although it was still early, people were already heading for the air raid shelters or the underground for safety. After months of bombing every night, it had become almost routine. A group of brave kids were out though, pushing a pram loaded with whatever they found in the bombed houses. Most of what they'd gathered wouldn't have got a glance before the war, but now we had to make do and mend, everything was precious. Balanced on top of their haul were long pieces of wooden beams that once supported ceilings. It wasn't unusual to see kids with prams loaded with what they found, but I was surprised to see one of the lads had a live chicken under his arm. His family would have both firewood and eggs.

I spotted a bus in the distance and put out my arm, 'Talking of head injuries, have you heard anything from Edith? I wonder how much her Sidney is affected?'

The bus swerved round a pothole in the road and stopped a hundred yards from us. We ran towards it and climbed on. It smelled of cigarette smoke and sweat. Most people looked tired as if they'd just finished work, but a few were dressed up for a night out. We were somewhere in between. Out of our usual army uniform, we'd put on summer dresses and cardigans. After being bombed out twice, most of our clothes were Women's Voluntary Service donations, but we were grateful for them. We'd coloured our legs with gravy juice and drawn lines up the back of our calves to look like seams. Bronwyn had even done my hair in a wonderful Victory Roll using an old laddered stocking tucked inside the roll to keep it in place.

The conductor followed us to our seats, 'Where to, Ladies? Off to a dance tonight, are you?'

'We'd be a bit more dressed up than this if we were, Boyo,' Bronwyn said, handing him the fares. He cranked the handle on his ticket machine and gave us our tickets with a cheeky grin and a wink. 'Have a good time anyway.'

'We were talking about Sidney,' Bronwyn said, 'I wonder if we can do anything to help Edith. Let's hope it's not too bad. She's being very closed about it.'

I looked out the window as daylight slowly dimmed. It seemed as if we rarely saw London clearly. After weeks of bombing there was often dust in the air. It got on your chest and made you cough; it got in your eyes making them sore; and it stuck to your lipstick making it gritty. Then there were the smells - dust, burning, decay, broken sewers. Often I was so used to it all, I barely noticed it; other days I longed for normal life, although I hardly remembered what that was.

Ruth's street was one of the lucky ones - not being near the docks or major industry the German planes had left it alone. Not a single house was damaged. If it wasn't for the Barrage Balloons floating overhead, you'd believe there was no war on. Late spring flowers brightened the small front gardens, and between the houses we noticed Anderson shelters and neat vegetable patches. Just walking along the street was enough to reduce the stress we lived with every day.

Ruth's door was painted black, shiny with gleaming door knocker and letter-box. Through the front window we saw a vase of pink and yellow wild flowers and some ornaments on the windowsill.

'Come in, come in!' Ruth cried, hugging us both. 'Marion is already here and we are getting to know each other. It is so good to make some new friends. Oh dear, I hope you like my cooking. I always get nervous cooking for new people.'

The house was semi-detached, three bedrooms and an upstairs bathroom, although none of the rooms were big. It felt comfortable and welcoming, and the smell of cooking made my mouth water.

Marion sat by the window, drinking tea. She was paler than usual and had dark rings under her eyes. 'You look peaky,' I said, 'are you okay?'

'Just the time of the month,' she whispered, 'I'm alright.'

Ruth came in holding a steaming dish. 'Soup, Ladies. I thought we'd eat straight away in case the bombers get started again.'

We sat down and Ruth said a brief prayer before we tucked in. 'Traditionally we have chicken soup,' she said, 'but there's not a lot of chicken in this soup. My apologies.'

The soup was delicious, 'It's wonderful. Can I have the recipe?' I asked, and she glowed, 'I'll bring it to work on Monday! It's traditional for Jewish people to eat together on Friday evening. This is my first Friday without my children so I'm very glad you are here, my friends. And since my husband left...' there was an awkward pause, 'left for his work in Scotland, I'll have the house to myself. It's very strange.'

'But your children are safe, and that's the important thing, Sweetheart,' Marion said.

'Perhaps I should have let them go sooner, but it's been quite safe around here.'

She looked out of the window, 'Oh, the light is almost gone; I'd better put up the black-out blinds.'

As we helped her, I looked at the photos on her sideboard, 'Your children really are lovely, Ruth, but where's the photos of your husband?'

She carried on with what she was doing, her back to me,

'Ruben hates having his photo taken. Awkward man,' she said as if that was the end of the topic.

She collected the dirty dishes and came back from the kitchen with another steaming bowl. 'This is Chamin,' she said, putting the bowl down on the table. 'You'd call it a stew. It's meat, not a lot I'm afraid, potatoes, beans and barley. We often have it on the Sabbath.'

When we'd finished eating, and sat back feeling fuller than we had for a long time, Ruth clapped her hands, 'My friends, I have an announcement to make. I hope you won't think I'm a silly woman.'

She smiled broadly, 'I have decided to join the Women's Voluntary Service! The government wants us to use our spare time to help. I've been looking at the options.'

I patted my stomach, 'I hope you're going to volunteer to cook. You're a natural.'

She laughed, 'Not a natural, my dear. Just someone with years of practice. But yes, I thought I would join one of the feeding stations or help in a British Restaurant. It will be better than sitting here on my own when I'm not at the Depot.'

'What about kosher food?' Marion asked, 'won't that be awkward for you?'

'I'm not that strict, my dear, and I don't expect everyone to follow the rules of my religion. In times like these we do what we can.'

Bronwyn stood up and started singing 'For she's a very good fellow,' and we all joined in. Ruth beamed with pleasure.

'Actually, I've got an announcement, too,' Bronwyn said, 'and it's about how I'll spend my spare time now my leg is all healed.'

'When you're not out dating!' I laughed.

She pretended to hit me round the head, 'Oy, you, never

mind your cheek. I'm going to be an ambulance driver. Just signed up today!'

'What, after you fell off your motorbike?' I teased, 'I bet you didn't tell them about that!'

Bronwyn put her hands on her hips, 'What they don't know, won't harm them. Anyway, driving an ambulance is different. A lot safer. Barring bombs; potholes, and incendiaries that is. And I'll be working with ARP people like you. They have a crew for each shift. Let's see if we can be in the same crew, Lily!'

Ruth pulled out a bottle of port - well - half a bottle of port. 'We can have a tiny sip of this to celebrate ourselves, Girls! And Bronwyn, if you're ever driving your ambulance near one of my feeding stations it'll be an extra helping for you!'

We raised the little glasses of amber liquid and toasted ourselves. 'To our health.' I noticed Marion looked more serious than the rest of us and wondered if she had pain from her monthly.

'Hey, Lily,' Marion said, 'You never did tell us how Edward got back to England after he'd been missing so long.'

I took a deep breath, 'It's a long story, but I'll give you the short version. He was badly injured and left for dead, but luckily a farmer and his wife took him in. They nursed him back to health, but it took ages. He couldn't remember who he was either.'

'Didn't the Germans come poking round?' she asked, 'surely they'd have spotted from his accent he wasn't French.'

'They got round that by pretending he couldn't speak. Anyway, when he was well enough they found some resistance people who got him out. Mind you, he had to walk over the Pyrenees. With a gammy leg and a walking stick!'

Ruth shook her head, 'Poor man, he must have been in so much pain. Is he properly healed now?'

'He's well enough to be doing a desk job so at least he feels useful.'

The rest of the evening passed with general chatter and Marion doing some crazy impersonations of Mr Lynch, our supervisor. 'Quiet now, Girls. I say, less noise if you don't mind. Cluck, cluck, cluck,' she squatted down and flapped her elbows like a chicken, making us all laugh.

The three of us walked back to the bus stop. Despite the dull sound of traffic from the big road nearby, our footsteps echoed on the pavements. With the total blackout we wouldn't have even been able to see our feet without our torches. In some ways we longed for moonlit nights so we could see where we were going and were less likely to have an accident. Trouble was, the moonlight made it easier for the German pilots to see where to bomb.

'Where do you live, Marion? I've just realised you've never mentioned it.'

She grunted, 'Not far, a few stops on the tube. Not that the tube will be working this time of night with everyone sleeping in them. Bus for me tonight.'

I couldn't see her in the blackout, but heard distress in her voice, 'Are you okay, Marion? You sound fed-up.'

'Oh, it's nothing, just the usual at home. My old man, my dad if you can call him that, is a pig and my mum never stands up to him. Nothing a lot of people don't have to put up with. Boyfriend trouble too.'

We were getting closer to the main road where there was more traffic, and had to take care not to accidentally step off the pavement when we couldn't see the edges. The white painted lines didn't show up unless you shone your torch directly onto them.

'That sounds miserable, Marion, is there anything we can do to help?'

'Tell you what I'd love. If you're going to the flicks any time, can I come with you?'

We walked past a pub, 'Why don't we go in?' Bronwyn said, 'it's not late and the buses will be running for ages yet. Mind you, now beer's gone up to eleven pence a pint, I'm only having the one.'

Like a lot of pubs, this one was run by a woman. Many men who used to run them were away at war. We quickly closed the door behind us to stop light showing through, pushed through the heavy curtain and walked to the bar. The air was thick with cigarette smoke, and the wooden floorboards were sticky.

'What can I get you, Girls?' the landlady asked, 'it's quiet tonight for a Friday. Wish we could have an army base or something round here.' she dropped her voice, 'apart from anything else it would lower the average age of my customers.'

We looked around. She was right. Such customers as there were were mostly elderly people hugging their drinks. Some played dominoes or cards, and in the other bar we heard thumping as darts hit a board. 'Good job we're not on the lookout for a beau!' Bronwyn said with a chuckle.

We sat down and sipped our beers. 'Why don't you go to the flicks with your boyfriend?' Bronwyn asked Marion, 'Has he been posted away?'

Marion tucked her hair behind her ears and looked into her drink, 'He's not my boyfriend any more, we've split up.'

There was silence while we waited for her to say more, but she didn't despite usually being more chatty.

'I'm sorry to hear about that,' I said finally, 'I'm guessing it wasn't your idea.'

She pulled her lips into a tight line, 'No, it wasn't. I thought we had something going between us. He thought otherwise, the so-and-so.'

'Oh well, what I always say is, plenty more fish in the sea. I'm fishing for a new lad at the moment,' Bronwyn said, 'maybe we can go fishing together. No good asking goody-two-shoes Lily here.'

An older man came up to our table. He had one arm in a sling; probably a veteran from the 1914-18 war. 'Can I get you Sweethearts another drink?' he asked. His meaning was clear.

'Not being funny nor nothing, but no thanks. We're happy as we are,' Bronwyn said without looking at him.

He wrinkled his nose and walked off without another word.

'I'm not really in the mood for fishing at the moment,' Marion said, 'but thanks for asking.'

'I guess life's hard for most of us, war or no war,' I said, 'You said things were difficult at home. Mine used to be. My dad was a miserable bully and a womaniser to boot. Best day of my life when he moved out. Then he got called up. Do him good.'

Marion turned to Bronwyn, 'What about you? Are your family okay?'

Bronwyn spluttered and sprayed her mouthful of beer on the table. 'I wish. Dirt poor; too many kids; not enough space; not enough food... want me to go on?'

Marion shook her head, 'No, I get the picture. But talking of that, let's go to the flicks one day next week. It'll cheer me up.'

'So, have you got a girlfriend then, Mr Lynch?' Bronwyn asked him next morning when we were having a tea break.

He went pink and fiddled with his tie, 'You think I don't get enough of girls with listening to you lot all day? It's enough to put any man off.'

Bronwyn laughed, 'You mean girls aren't your thing, then?'

He slammed his hand on his desk, 'I mean I have enough listening to your tittle-tattle every day. Then I go home to listen to my mother's. Sometimes all a man wants is a bit of quiet to read a book,' he stood up, 'right, break over. Back to typing if you don't mind, Girls.'

Bronwyn looked at me, gave a little smile and raised an eyebrow.

As I turned to leave the room I glanced out of the window and saw creepy Mr Biggerstaff going into one of the warehouses. After I solved the mystery of the depot theft before, Mr McDonald told me to keep an eye on anyone I thought was dodgy. I picked up one of the invoices I was about to type, 'Just going to check a discrepancy.' I muttered and headed for the door. Mr Lynch was engrossed in some figure work and didn't even look up.

Walking as quietly as possible in army shoes, I headed to the warehouse hoping the background noise would cover my footsteps. I stopped just outside the doorway and tried to listen, but it was hopeless. A lorry came into the yard; a train pulled into the station nearby, its whistle announcing its approach; men grunted as they moved big boxes around.

I had to go for it.

I walked in and said a cheery 'hello' to the nearest man, trying not to obviously look at Mr Biggerstaff. I needn't have worried; he was at the back of the warehouse deep in conversation with one of the men whose name I thought was Jimmy. Jimmy was an older man, as many of them were; most younger men were away at war. He hadn't a hair on his head which accentuated the ugly lump on his forehead. People sometimes say that you were born with the face God gave you, but by the time you were forty you had the face you deserve. His face spoke of hardship and mistrust.

It was easy to invent an excuse to walk towards them. I held the invoice in front of me and pretended to be checking it against the stock on the shelf. The whole time I was trying to listen to their conversation over the background noise.

By the time I got close enough to hear them, they were winding up. 'So you've got that clear then?' Mr Biggerstaff was saying.

'I told you I have!' Jimmy said, with an edge to his voice.

Mr Biggerstaff turned to leave and then saw me. His frown changed to a tight smile. 'I didn't see you there,' he said, 'wait a minute, didn't we meet the first time I came here?'

'We did,' I thought about holding out my hand to shake

his, but decided he was the type of man who'd think I was a pushy woman. I didn't want to be on his radar; better to be the mousy type he'd ignore. I nodded and walked on, looking again at the shelves, but I wondered why he was giving Jimmy orders. Jimmy couldn't work for him legitimately during Depot hours. That meant it had to be something on the side. Perhaps he was working for Biggerstaff after work, or perhaps they were up to something with Depot stock.

❧

Back in the building Mr Lynch's phone rang. He said a few words then looked up. 'Bronwyn! Lily! Mr McDonald wants to see you now. I hope you haven't been up to any mischief.' He gave a little chuckle as he usually did when he thought he'd said something funny.

I was tempted to stick my tongue out at him. Instead I walked calmly out of the door like a grown-up. As soon as we were outside the door Bronwyn and I turned round and made daft rude gestures to him, safe in the knowledge he couldn't see us.

'Tell the truth now,' Bronwyn said as we walked along the corridor, 'he's not a bad boss. Bit useless, but we've had worse.'

'Still living with his mum at his age though!' I said unkindly, especially as accommodation was so hard to find. 'I wonder what Mr McDonald wants. We haven't done anything wrong, have we?'

Bronwyn pretended to polish her halo, 'I don't know what you've been up to, but I've been good as gold, I have.'

We knocked and went in. Mr McDonald was finishing a cup of tea. He wiped his mouth on a spotless white hanky. 'Excuse me girls, late lunch. Do sit down.'

He waited for us to be seated, 'I've got a very unusual offer for you. Very unusual indeed. Nothing to do directly with war. Instead it might be an offer you'll like very much. Yes, indeed.'

He sat back and steepled his fingers as if he'd already told us what it was and was waiting for an answer. I thought he was going to nod off.

After a pause I said, 'What is the offer, Mr McDonald?'

He shook himself as if from a post-meal snooze, 'Silly me, I haven't told you. Well, it very occasionally happens that houses belonging to army officers are empty for a while. They're posted abroad or to another part of the country and there is no-one else to keep an eye on the place. Sometimes they get a housekeeper in, but some of them can't afford that.'

Another pause. I had no idea what that had to do with us.

'Anyway, I've been made aware of just such a property. It's in a good part of town; a posh part, a biggish house, split into three flats, but in a dilapidated state. The owner already has one couple living in the upstairs section and is looking for two more people for downstairs. The basement is not fit for human habitation. It's a peppercorn rent although there would still be bills to pay, of course. I know you've been bombed out a couple of times, and I trust you not to wreck the place.'

He pushed a piece of paper towards us with the address on it. I was about to ask for more details when Bronwyn nudged me aside. 'We'll take it! What do we have to do?'

'You have to look after the property, make sure it doesn't deteriorate any further. If any repairs are needed you'd check with the owner, then get them done if he gives you the go ahead. Naturally, if it were bombed you would not be held responsible.'

'I bloody hope not!' Bronwyn muttered. He pretended not to hear.

He sat back again resting his hands on his round stomach. 'I think the best thing you can do is go and meet the couple who are already there. If you don't think you'd like them, it will be better to stay where you are. You've got the address, so it's up to you to go to meet them. If you think you'll get on with them I'll sort out the necessary paperwork. Let me know soon either way because if you don't want it I'll find someone else to offer it to.'

We stepped outside his door and looked at each other in disbelief. Then we did a silly happy dance on the spot.

'A biggish house!'

'Peppercorn rent!'

'Posh area!'

I turned to Bronwyn, 'Is it? A posh area? I don't know it.'

She grinned, 'It's tidy, it really is. I used to ride my motor-bike through there sometimes and I always looked at the houses and wished I was one of the lucky beggars living in them. Now I, we, will be!'

The house was in Bloomsbury, seven miles away from the Depot so too far to walk, especially with so much disruption in the roads. We decided to go straight from work and go by bus.

'Let's stop on the way and get a bite to eat,' Bronwyn suggested.

We had to change busses about halfway there and quickly found a little cafe near the bus stop. 'I fancy an egg banjo sandwich,' she said.

'You what? Whatever's that? Do you eat it or play it?'

'You must have had one. It's a fried egg sandwich with

loads of ketchup. It was one of the few things my mum could cook.'

I thought back to what my mum cooked: corned beef hash, spam fritters, Lord Woolton's pie, carrot scones, potato piglets and lots more - and egg sandwiches. My mouth watered thinking about it. We were poor, but we never went to bed hungry.

The cafe was packed with workers looking tired after a day's work. They turned to look at us in our uniforms and someone wolf-whistled.

We sat at the table, and a young waitress with dark rings under her eyes came and took our order. I looked around and was surprised to spot one of our warehousemen two tables away. He saw me and waved. I waved back, then he came over.

'Fancy seeing you here, Love. Do you live in this neck of the woods?'

Bronwyn kicked my ankle, 'No,' she said, 'we're on our way to visit a friend. You live near here?'

'Not far. Just got a delivery to do on the way home then I'm done for the day.'

Our warehousemen weren't expected to do deliveries. 'What are you delivering then? Must be a rush order.'

He shrugged, 'Dunno, to tell you the truth. Jimmy what works with me asked me to deliver it to... he took a creased and greasy piece of paper out of his pocket, 'a Mr Biggerstaff. He's got an office round here somewhere. I'll go when I've finished my cuppa.'

'Why isn't Jimmy delivering it himself?' I asked.

'You're a nosy one, ain't ya? Jimmy said he had something else on. All gotta help each other out these days, ain't we?' he turned away, 'Have a good evening, girls.'

'Isn't that Biggerstaff the one you're keeping an eye on?' Bronwyn asked, dousing her egg sandwich in yet more sauce.

'He is, but I don't know what we can make of that delivery. He might have just left something behind when he was in the warehouse last time.'

Bronwyn wrinkled her nose, 'I smell something dodgy, and it's not this cheap brown sauce. Mam used to say if it walks like a duck and quacks like a duck then it probably is a duck. He's up to something.'

I kept an eye out to see if the size of the parcel gave anything away, but it was an innocent looking box about the size of a shoe box.

'Any ideas?' I asked her, nodding towards the parcel.

'Shoes? Cigarettes? Hundreds of pound notes? Might be anything.'

We got off the second bus and walked towards the house in Bloomsbury, gaping like tourists. The people we passed wore expensive clothes or officers' uniforms. A nanny in a green uniform with a starched white collar pushed a big expensive pram, her back straighter than any army officer. The trees in the square opposite the house were dressed in light green. Unlike much of London where railings had been removed to be melted for war use, the railings round the pretty square were still intact, as shiny as if a skivvy had polished them that morning.

Although the houses were joined, no-one would call them terraced houses; they were far too elegant. I'd seen pictures of them in books and thought they might be Georgian. I got the key out of my bag as we approached the right number. The stairs to the basement were part of the tiny front garden.

Weeds came through cracks there making the house look more neglected than its neighbours. Four steps led up to the front door which was painted dark blue with a brass knocker in the shape of a lion's head.

I was just about to put the key in the door when it opened and I almost fell forward into it. The first thing I saw was some highly polished army shoes.

'Who the hell are you?' the man said, voice harsh enough to grate stale cheese, 'and what are you doing with that key? Give it to me immediately!' he held out his hand.

By now I was upright. I automatically saluted because he was an officer. But although I'd had it drilled into me to always obey orders from officers, there was no way I was going to obey this one.

'We're here to look at the rooms. It's official.'

His eyes narrowed, making them look even smaller in his pudgy face. 'Who sent you?'

Bronwyn stepped up so she was level with me. She held out her hand as if to shake his, 'Nice to meet you. I'm Bronwyn Jones, and this is Lily Baker. We work at the Depot in Deptford.'

He ignored her out hand, but instead looked at his watch. 'This is most irregular. We shouldn't be expected to share premises with the lower ranks!' he looked pointedly at Bronwyn, 'especially lower ranks like you!'

And with that he marched off as if he was on a parade ground.

'Well, he doesn't like the colour of my skin,' Bronwyn said, 'but I've dealt with worse.'

'That's just awful, Bron,' I said, so outraged I could barely breathe, 'I'll defend you. He's just ignorant.'

'Ignorant and a pig. I'm glad he's not our boss,' Bronwyn muttered, pulling a face at his retreating back.

We walked into the hall which stretched forever. The wallpaper was old fashioned and a bit marked, but not falling down much. Nothing that a bit of paste wouldn't fix. We stepped into the first room; it was enormous. Most of the floor was bare boards, but there was a threadbare rug in faded pink and cream in the middle of the room. You could have fitted the rooms we had now into just that one room. The windows were tall, although light from them was limited by the inevitable paper crosses in case of bomb blast. There was a fair bit of grime on them, too.

I looked at Bronwyn, 'Mr McDonald did say we can have the ground floor, didn't he?' I whispered, feeling as if I was in someone else's life.

'He certainly did,' she said and proceeded to walk around prodding walls and stamping on the floorboards. 'Well, it's tidy, really tidy. We can soon brighten up these sticks of furniture with secondhand bedspreads from the market or a jumble sale. We'll get housemaids knee cleaning the place first, but we've had to do that most places we've lived.'

She wasn't wrong about the furniture. There were two high backed maroon upholstered chairs, both almost thread-bare, a sideboard and a coffee table. In a room that size they looked like doll's house furniture.

'Come on,' I said, grabbing her hand, 'let's look at the other rooms.'

There was a dining room, only slightly smaller, with a tatty dining table and three tired dining chairs. In the corner was a tall pile of newspapers.

'That front room will be our bedroom,' I said, ' we don't want to have to walk through it to get to the kitchen and bath-room, do we? And we need to get to the market and see if we can get some second-hand beds.'

'We can always sleep on the floor if need be. It wouldn't be for ever.'

The next room was the kitchen. It was really old fashioned with an ancient cooker and a wonky table. The sink was cracked and when I turned on the tap it spluttered, then grey water splurged out of it. I let it run for a minute to see if the sink leaked, but the water gradually cleared and there were no tell-tale puddles on the floor.

'It'll do!' I said, 'it'll be tip-top in no time.'

The last room was the bathroom. The bath was grey and spotted with age and the toilet needed a damn good scrub, but it was a big improvement on having to share a bathroom like we'd been used to.

We went out into the garden and found an outside lavvy. I opened the door and closed it again quickly. A million spiders had made it their home. ''This'll be useful if one of us is in the bath. Two lavvies, what a luxury!'

'You can have the one with the spiders,' I said, grimacing.

'I'm not joking nor nothing, but that's nothing compared to what we had to put up with in Swansea.'

I remembered the newspapers in the dining room. We wouldn't be short of paper to cut up to use in the toilets.

The garden was a jungle; brambles and weeds everywhere. I remembered how Mum had turned our back garden in the new place into somewhere lovely despite having to clear a lot of builder's rubbish. 'We can grow our own veg!' I said, 'someone at work will tell us how. Maybe get a couple of chickens for some eggs.'

Bronwyn smiled, 'You're always good for a laugh. It'll be Christmas before we clear this lot!' she turned back towards the house, 'come on, let's go and tell our landlady we're leaving.'

*M*r Lynch was out of the office so we were chatting about which film we'd like to see that evening without having to worry about him moaning. 'What do you fancy?' I asked.

We looked in the newspaper and decided on *This England*. 'It's not a new one but it looks good,' Edith said, 'fancy following one village from the Norman Conquest. What a story that village could tell. Any village, I suppose. All those births, marriages and deaths. Not to mention people getting up to things they shouldn't do,' she went quiet for a minute, 'I think I'll come with you all, if you don't mind. Sidney's mum will sit with him. She pops in every day anyway.'

'I can't go,' Ruth said, 'it's my first night with the WVS. I'm hoping to make some new friends.'

'We not good enough for you then?' Bronwyn teased.

Ruth blushed, and fiddled with the button on the top of her blouse, 'No, silly. I love working here with you lot, but it will be nice to make some friends my own age, too.'

'But surely you and your husband must have friends.'

'Of course we do, but then we moved, so it's like having to start all over again.'

I looked at the clock on the wall. 'It's almost knocking off time. I don't think Mr Lynch is going to be back today.'

As I put the cover on my typewriter, a movement outside caught my eye. It was Mr Biggerstaff again. I picked up one of the invoices in my in-tray, 'Just got to check this before I go. Won't be a minute. Wait for me!'

Buttoning up my jacket I headed outside. Pretending to be in a hurry to get to one of the warehouses, I rushed past Mr Biggerstaff and deliberately dropped the paper near him. As I hoped, he picked it up and handed it to me.

'We met before, didn't we?' he said with a silky smile, 'you're...'

'Lily. Lily Baker. I work in the office and we've met twice before. I just wanted to check this invoice, but I suppose it can wait until tomorrow. Trouble is, in a depot like this, things go missing and it's hard to know if there's been a mistake or if someone is stealing stuff.' I hoped to get some reaction from him - a guilty look or something, but there was nothing.

I was just about to reply when Bronwyn appeared at my side. She looked at Mr Biggerstaff, and held out her hand to shake his. She looked very forward. 'Hello, it's Mr Biggerstaff, isn't it? I work with Lily and I think you and I met before.'

He held her hand a fraction too long and winked at her very quickly, too. I frowned and wondered if they were secretly up to something.

'I'd love to stop to chat, Girls,' he said, 'but time is short. I hope you have a good evening.' He tipped his hat and walked briskly into the nearest warehouse.

Marion and Edith were waiting for us at the gate, so I

couldn't say much then, but my raised eyebrow told Bronwyn we needed to have a chat.

～

I bumped into Biggerstaff again a few days later. It was amazing how often he found reasons to visit the depot. When he saw me, he stopped what he was doing and came up to me, a smarmy smile on his face, 'I'm glad I bumped into you, I've been wanting a word. Have you got a minute?'

I nodded, wondering what was coming.

'You're a smart girl,' he said, leading me towards a pile of pallets, 'let's sit down here.' He wore his usual suit and tie, his hair slicked back with oil. His pudgy fingers had well-manicured nails.

'I started to say, I've heard you're a smart girl,' he paused and I had no idea how to answer that.

'Did you want something? Is everything okay with the paperwork?'

'The paperwork is spot on, I'd let you know if there was a problem. No, it's not about work. It's like this, I know you girls don't earn very much.'

That was true. We didn't earn as much as male soldiers.

'So I was wondering,' he went on, 'if you'd like to do a spot of work for me in your spare time.'

My immediate instinct was to laugh; between work and ARP duties, I had precious little spare time. Added to that, I found him creepy. But I bit back the words. The money would be useful, and it would give me a chance to find out if he was up to something.

'What sort of work do you mean?' I asked.

'This and that, you know.'

I shook my head, 'No, I don't know. What do you mean?'

'Pass messages on to people. Keep your eyes and ears open here. That sort of thing.'

'Why would you need messages passed on? Can't you write to people, or phone, or find a lad who wants to earn a few pennies?'

It was his turn to shake his head, 'No, I need someone reliable; someone sharp witted. It'd only be occasional, not a regular thing. I've got several businesses and don't have time to do everything myself.'

'I'm not sure,' I said with a frown, 'is any of this dodgy? I won't do anything illegal.'

He smiled, and the smile reminded me of a wolf in fairy tales. 'I would never ask you to do that. It's just helping me out, providing a bit of information. You don't have to do anything you don't want to do. You can always say no if you feel uncomfortable. What do you think? Is it a deal?'

He held out his hand to shake mine. I took it. What else could I do? But inside I was shaking, wondering what I was letting myself in for.

~

First thing next morning I went to see Mr McDonald.

'Come in!' he called when I knocked.

'Have you got a minute, Sir?' I asked, clearing my throat.

'Sit down, Lily. You know I've always got time for you. What is it?'

I sat on the edge on the seat and wiped my damp palms on my skirt, 'Something strange happened yesterday. Mr Biggerstaff asked if I wanted to do some private work for him. I

34

don't... well to be honest...' I stopped, wondering if I'd look stupid with what I wanted to say.

'Come on Lily, out with it. You don't what...?'

'I don't trust him. My instincts aren't always right, but they often are.'

He sat back and steepled his fingers. 'Hmm, let me think. Your instinct is that Mr Biggerstaff is up to something.' He sat without speaking for a minute or two. 'You'll have seen warehouse two is now secure. I expect it's an open secret that we're storing more dangerous goods in there.'

'Guns, I heard.'

'That would be an official secret, so I can't say. But if your instincts are right, this may be very serious.' He paused for a little while looking down at his hands, 'I'd like to make a suggestion. Just for now would you play along with it. My guess is he'll give you something innocent to do for the first time or two. He'll want something he can hold over you when he wants you to do something more serious.'

My heart sank, 'Blackmail, you mean?'

'Yes, blackmail. But you and I will be working together, so if he threatens you with telling me what you've been doing, his threat won't work. Are you happy to try that for a little while until we can see what he's up to?'

'I suppose so, as long as I can tell you each time he contacts me. And I want to be able to stop at any time.'

'That sounds just the ticket. I know he visits the Depot a lot more often than other suppliers, although he always has some reason why. This is the first bit of proof he's up to something. Keep me fully in the picture and it should all be okay.'

If only he'd been right.

$\mathcal{T}$he film was a bit dull, and I was glad when the house lights went up. But not so glad when the air raid sirens blared at the same time. Like most people, we'd got a bit careless if the sirens went off in the middle of the film. We often stayed where we were and hoped for the best. But now, well into the evening, we decided to head for a shelter. It was a bomber's moon - cloudless sky with a moon so bright you could forget the blackout and using shielded torches. We hurried, following everyone else and hoping they knew where a shelter was; we weren't near enough to an underground station to get to one quickly.

As we walked, we spotted an alleyway and a lady indicated to us to go in. She was pointing behind her. We ran into the alley and discovered she was pointing to an Anderson shelter, but when she realised there were four of us she shook her head, 'Not enough room!' she shouted over the siren blare. We ran back down the alley and followed the crowd, still with no idea where we were going.

It was a communal air raid shelter. People were almost tripping over each other in their eagerness to get to safety.

'Hurry up!' 'Mind my toes!' 'Help Mum!' 'What the hell did you bring the budgie for!' and loads of other commands overlapped as we pushed forward. I was last of us four, and I'd only got two or three steps in when there was an almighty swoosh of air and I was thumped in the back by the shelter door which was blown open but still on its hinges. The force of the explosion made the stale air of the shelter mingle with dust, little bits of brick and wood, and rubbish all blown in. The jolt knocked me off my feet and I fell on Edith, who fell on Marion, and before you knew it it was like a set of dominoes with everyone knocking everyone else over.

There was pandemonium; a lot of screaming and shouting, as well as people pushing each other as they tried to get upright.

'My baby! My baby!' someone shouted, then someone hushed her saying, 'he's okay. Look, nothing broken! Calm down!'

A man called out, 'My head's bleeding - a lot!' A woman near him said, 'Let me look, I've had some first aid training.' With my ARP training I could have helped him myself, but I wasn't close enough.

'The budgie's escaped!' someone cried and I felt it fly past my head on its way to freedom. I wondered how on earth something so small and fragile could have survived the massive rush of air.

I was a bit dazed, but like the baby had no broken bones although I could feel a bump coming up on my head. I dreaded to think what had happened to the Air Raid volunteer who showed us in. There was no way he could have survived that blast unscathed, and I felt overwhelming sadness for him and those who loved him. His probable end made me go cold. That could have been me if it was my night on duty. Us Air Raid Protection wardens rarely talked about the danger, yet we were all aware of it. You had to be an optimist to volunteer for that job, hoping you'd end every shift alive and in one piece. We all knew someone who had been injured or died while on duty.

Without the door we could see moonlight again through the doorway as the dust drifted away. Very quickly another ARP warden and a police officer were ushering us out.

'Come on!' they shouted, 'siren's stopped, but it could start again any minute.' I hadn't even noticed it had stopped because of the ringing noise in my ears.

'What was that?' I asked as I went past the policeman, 'I didn't hear a bomb go off.'

'Parachute bomb,' he said, 'go on now, get to the Rest Station in Goodman's Road. They'll be expecting you. Give your name to the warden over there before you go.'

A lot slower now, we all plodded along to Goodman's Road, only about a quarter of a mile away. It felt like I'd gained five stones in those few minutes; my feet dragged as if stuck by magnets to the road, and my head and ears felt stuffed with cotton wool. The air was still full of dust that got in our eyes and made us cough. The ringing of fire engines and ambulances competed with the sounds of falling bricks and timber as well as emergency workers calling instructions to each other. A couple of fires broke out, probably from broken gas pipes. Three people scrabbled dangerously through the debris of houses that were standing just minutes before. I wondered if they were looters, or if they were searching their own homes for any of their belongings. Then we saw the bodies; the people who were behind us as we hurried to the shelter. They didn't make it to safety. They lay, limbs at impossible angles. Not all the bodies were intact and people cried out as they passed an arm or a leg with no body attached. I'd seen that several times before, even had to deal with it, but it still broke my heart and made me want to weep. I trembled as I staggered past.

A minute later I glanced down the alleyway we'd run into, and put my hands over my mouth to hold back a scream. The rear of the house in front of the shelter and the shelter itself were totally flattened. Men were frantically trying to rescue people; throwing aside bricks, broken glass and wood with torn and bleeding hands. But no-one could have survived that. I said a prayer for them and sent one up in thanks that we hadn't gone in there with them. Unlike them, we'd had a lucky escape.

Eventually we reached the church hall. The warden who had been leading us like lost sheep, indicated to go inside, 'Get yourself a cuppa and a bit of floor to sleep on,' he said.

As an ARP warden, I was well used to the brisk kindness of Women's Voluntary Service ladies, but that night I was more glad to see them than ever. They stood behind long tables laden with slices of bread and marge and poured strong tea out of enormous metal teapots. Along with my colleagues I sat on the floor holding my cup and saucer, but too bombed out mentally to even drink it before it got cold. None of us said a word. After a while we gave our cups to the WVS ladies who were coming round with blankets, and lay down. Not that we slept. We were still in a state of shock, I supposed some people would call it shell-shocked. I lay with eyes unwilling to close. Because of the blackout the only light was when new people arrived and the door was briefly opened, or when people lit their cigarettes. But the darkness didn't make sleep any easier. My mind was full of the images of the dead and dying we had passed. Other people were restless too, I heard groans and sighs; a baby fretting; sneezes and whispered conversations.

I had no idea what time it was when I turned over towards

Edith, and discovered her laying wide awake. I smiled, although I wasn't sure if she could see me enough to know that.

She shifted her position, 'Can I tell you something?' she whispered, 'it's very private. You can't tell anyone else.'

My heart sank; this wasn't going to be anything good. 'Of course,' I said, 'I can keep a secret.'

The door opened as someone new came in and we stopped talking while they got settled in.

'It's about Sidney,' she whispered, 'it's since he came back from the war.'

I waited. Sometimes saying nothing was better than speaking.

'He's not the same,' she said, and sobbed, 'he's a different man.'

I frowned, 'What do you mean, different?'

She wiped her eyes, 'You know he used to be a lovely kind man. He's like, well, like he's empty inside. He sits doing nothing a lot of the time. The only time he seems to come alive is when his niece and nephews come round. Me and his mum don't know what to do. And that's not all... he can't...'

'Ssshhh,' someone whispered, much more loudly than we were speaking.

We were silent for a couple of minutes then, 'Can I talk to you about it tomorrow?' she asked.

I reached out and held her hand, 'Whenever you like, you know that!'

She squeezed my hand, then let go. I figured it would soon be dawn, very early at that time of year. I managed to sleep, but woke when people started to stir ready for work or back home. I wondered if our home would still be standing.

CHAPTER 6

'*H*alf price for you ladies in uniform.' The elderly man at the door gave us a toothless smile; handed us our tickets, winked, and sent us into the dance hall.

The Roxy was packed as usual. We gave our coats to the cloakroom girl and walked in through a wall of noise and cigarette smoke. The band was playing *I don't want to set the world on fire*, a new song I'd only heard once before on the wireless. Although it was quite a slow number, couples still managed to jive to it - those that weren't smooching, anyway. Most of the men were in uniform and no doubt home on leave. A mirror ball sent sparkles all around the room and some glinted off the brass instruments on the stage.

Although the doors had opened a mere thirty minutes earlier, a lot of dancers already had damp patches under their arms.

The four of us pushed our way through to the bar. Me and Bronwyn were surprised Edith wanted to come. It seemed like she took every opportunity for a night out despite her Sidney being not long back from the war.

We got ourselves some cider and grabbed a tiny table and

four chairs at the back of the room. 'You going to dance tonight?' Marion asked us all.

'Why else would we come?' Edith said, her voice sharp. In the office she'd been quieter than usual, and her skin, normally smooth and glowing, looked lacklustre. It was obvious something was bothering her, but she wasn't saying what.

'How's Sidney now?' I asked,

She took a long swig of her cider, 'It takes time.' She looked around, 'shall we go and dance or wait to be asked?'

She didn't have to wait long. Within five minutes we were all dancing. My fiancé Edward knew that I went to dances occasionally and he'd never said he minded.

After a few dances, we needed to get some fresh air so we went out the back. It was a narrow back lane, barely big enough for the brewery lorries when they delivered their beer. A couple were necking, squashed up against a wall. Another couple were smoking and chatting, the girl fanning herself. It was a lovely late spring evening; the air was cool and twilight was beginning. There'd been no bombing for a few nights and we all hoped that was the end of it.

'How is your ARP work going?' Marion asked.

'The Incendiaries keep us busy, wretched things. Trouble is, you don't hear them coming and when they do, there's so many of them we can't keep up with putting them all out. Thank goodness some of them fall on the road. If they all fell on houses there'd be nowhere left. I spent hours on a church roof last week putting out little fires before they could spread.'

'Rather you than me,' Marion said, 'especially when you've been injured before.'

I was glad when a chill breeze ran over us and we decided to go in. I tried not to think of the awful night when I nearly died and the wonderful man I was on duty with passed away. I touched the small scar on my forehead without thinking - a permanent reminder of that dreadful night when a bomb blast knocked me unconscious.

'Hey!' Bronwyn said, making us all jump, 'me and Lily haven't told you our good news!'

Edith and Marion looked at her and then at me, 'We couldn't tell you before it was all sorted, but we've got somewhere better to live.'

'You weren't bombed out again, were you?' Edith asked.

'No, Mr McDonald found us a sort of house-sitting place. Half a house that belongs to an officer who's away.'

Marion frowned, 'I don't understand. You're going to live in half a house? What do you have to do for it? Who will you share with?'

They were agog at our story and insisted we invite them round to tea the next week.

'Come on, let's go back in,' Bronwyn said, wrapping her arms round herself against the breeze.

As Edith and Bronwyn stepped ahead of us, Marion pulled me back, 'Can I talk to you a minute?'

I really wanted to go in to get out of the chill, but she looked worried. 'What is it Marion? You look like you want to cry. Has something dreadful happened?

She gulped, and put her hands to her stomach, 'I'm in the family way, up the duff, and my rotten boyfriend has dumped me.'

Her problem made me catch my breath, 'Oh Marion, that's terrible. Have you told your folks yet?'

'No, I'm too scared. I'm not showing yet or my dad would have thrown me out. Tell you the truth, I'm trying not to think about it.'

My heart went out to her, 'Any time you want to talk about it, just let me know. I'll do anything I can to help.'

She wiped a tear from her eye, 'Thanks Lily, I'm so worried I'm hardly sleeping.'

I put my hand on hers, 'Have you thought about a mother-and-baby home? You could go to one in another part of the country. Then if you have the baby adopted, no-one would know you'd ever had one. You could carry on with your life.'

She gave a bitter laugh, 'My life will never be the same. Whether I keep the baby, or I give it up, my life is changed for ever.'

'No word from your ex-boyfriend, I suppose?'

She took a deep breath, 'No, but I plucked up courage and wrote to his Commanding Officer explaining what had happened. I'm still waiting for a reply.'

'That was a good idea. Let's hope it helps.'

A week later Bronwyn and I staggered up the steps to our new home, arms full of our meagre belongings. After being bombed out twice, we didn't own much. But we'd been to a jumble sale and several markets and gradually stocked the rooms with the essentials. We had second-hand mattresses; pillows; bedding; and cooking equipment. Every minute of our spare time had been spent scrubbing the rooms until they sparkled.

After what seemed like days, the wooden floor shone and most of the marks on the walls were a distant memory. The pile of newspapers was dusted off and each page torn into squares and put on metal spikes to use as toilet paper.

We heard footsteps coming down the stairs and the wife

of the misery guts we met on our first visit came in after knocking briefly.

'I hope you don't mind me walking in,' she said, 'I'm Wendy. I live upstairs and I've heard you coming and going. It was a bit of a shock because I didn't know anyone else would be sharing the house.'

'We did bump into your husband the other day. We share the main front door. but this is our own door.' I said as we introduced ourselves.

'Thomas?' she asked, 'He didn't say.'

She was a very thin woman. On wartime rations most people were thin but she was skeletal, and I wondered if she was ill. She had dark rings under her eyes and her skin was dull. But she was friendly. 'It'll be so nice to have some women in the place. I don't know anyone around here,' she said, 'you look busy, I'll make you a cup of tea.'

I wiped my hands on a cloth, 'No, sit down. This isn't a palace, but you can be our first guest. I'll get the kettle on.'

It took me a couple of minutes to remember where we'd put the tea and tinned milk, so I was glad Wendy made herself at home in an armchair. She was reading a three day old Daily Express that was destined for the lavvy as well.

'I don't often read the newspaper,' she said as I walked back in with the tea things, 'it makes me so depressed. But then Thomas gets cross if I don't keep up to date with what's happening in the war.'

I put the tray down on the battered coffee table, 'Do you listen to the news on the wireless?'

'Mmm, once a day. That's enough for me.'

We only owned four cups, all different. I poured her tea into the least cracked, 'I'm afraid we haven't got any sugar.'

She patted her hollow stomach, 'I never take sugar.

Thomas likes me to keep my figure. He's very proud of me, and when we go to officer's events, he likes to show me off.'

I thought she could be a good bit heavier and still look perfect.

Bronwyn walked in wiping her hands on the wraparound pinny she swore she'd never wear.

'I'll look like my old gran!' she'd moaned.

I got out of the other chair and sat on the floor. She fell into the one I'd vacated with a thud. 'Springs in this've seen better days.' she said, then turned to Wendy. 'Sorry, you've not caught me at my best. Not sure there is a best to be honest. But I wanted to ask if you know any of the neighbours yet.'

Wendy put down her cup. 'We haven't lived here long, but they look like a real mixed bunch. That side,' she pointed to the right, 'they're really up themselves. Even with Thomas looking so good in his officer's uniform, they looked down their noses at him. They didn't even say hello to me.'

'What about the other side?'

She smiled widely and the tension in her shoulders dropped, 'They couldn't be more different - Arty. Several of them live there, I'm not sure how many, there always seems too be people coming and going. Although they invited me in for a cup of tea, I couldn't work out the relationships between them. There are three women and two men. One of the men was writing a book - he told me he'd lost a leg in the Great War so wasn't called up this time. The others all seemed to be artists.'

I let that sink in, 'You mean they draw and paint all day? Don't they do their bit for the war effort?'

'I didn't like to ask, but they go out regularly so I think they must be doing something. You'll like them. And one of them,' she looked at Bronwyn, 'has hair just like yours, but lighter.'

And so we made a new friend. Her husband might be so stuffy he could have a stick up his back, but we looked forward to getting to know her better.

Before long we were to learn more about their relationship than we wanted to know.

CHAPTER 7

*E*dith and Marion joined me and Bronwyn on a trip to the flicks a few days later. For a while when the bombing starting the stupid government closed down the picture houses, but they soon realised their mistake and opened them again. We had plenty of films to choose from. After some debate we settled on *Gaslight*, a thriller starring Anton Walbrook and Diana Wynyard.

We went to the picture house nearest work, stopping first to have something to eat in Lyons Corner House. We no sooner sat down than a Nippy, looking very smart in her black and white uniform, came to take our order. The place was busy - we weren't the only ones who wanted to fill up before we went to the pictures.

'Egg on toast for me please, and a cup of tea.'

Soon she had all our orders taken down. She must have been worn out. The restaurant was massive, with regimented rows of tables almost as far as the eye could see. With so many people it was noisy and we had to speak loudly to hear each other.

Edith, who surprisingly had joined us, lit up a Woodbine.

'Anyone else want one?' she asked. Marion took one and soon they were enjoying their cigarettes although the room was already a bit hazy with the ciggie smoke.

'So what made you come this evening?' Bronwyn asked Edith, 'had enough of Sidney already?' she was joking of course, but Edith didn't smile.

'He doesn't mind. Remember I had that week off with him when he first got home. He's had me all to himself. This evening his mum is with him again.'

Someone leaned across from the next table, 'Can I borrow the salt?' the man said.

Marion passed it to him and he blew her a cheeky kiss.

'It must be strange getting to know each other all over again after him being away for so long.' Bronwyn said.

Edith rubbed an eyebrow, 'That's bound to happen, isn't it. To anyone. We miss them but get set in our ways, then they come home and we all have to make adjustments. It'll work out. Now, let's talk about other things. What do you know about the film?'

'It sounds tidy,' Bronwyn said, taking her meal from the Nippy who'd returned very quickly, 'a husband tries to convince his wife she's going crazy.'

'Sounds like the bloke my mum used to go out with,' I said, my heart sinking at the memories, 'he was an expert at twisting anything you said. He tried to get off with me when she wasn't looking. Mind you, she didn't believe me at first when I told her.'

Edith put down her knife and fork and looked at me, 'That's terrible, you must have been so hurt. Is your mother still with him?'

I looked down to cut up my toast, 'No, she only caught him in her bed with another woman, didn't she. She thought they looked like a couple of dogs at it so she threw a bowl of water over the pair of them.'

They all laughed so much, a couple of them choked, 'Wish I'd been there to see that.' Marion said when she could get her breath.

'Maybe not. Mum said he had a hairy bum!'

That set us off laughing again so much people in nearby tables turned to look at us.

I checked my watch, 'Come on girls, time we headed off.'

There was still some light outside which made life easier. There were plenty of people heading toward the picture house and we had to queue to get our tickets. We just got to our seats when we had to stand for the National Anthem. The B film was a silly horror and I fell asleep half way through, but Bronwyn nudged me in the interval to get some ice cream from the usherette.

We stood up to leave the picture house at the end of *Gaslight* when the Air Raid alarms sounded. Clutching our gas masks and handbags, we hurried out of the building and to the nearest Bomb Shelter under Burton's the Tailors in the High Street. ARP wardens ushered us and what seemed like half the film goers into the basement. The basement must have been bigger than the shop, so probably went under other shops. It was used as a store-room, but the stock had all been pushed against one wall and roped off.

Old mattresses and blankets covered the floor and in one corner there was a water boiler and the things needed to make tea. The walls had been painted white a long time ago, but showed the scratches and scars of age and frequent use. Old Burton's ads were propped against one wall, showing fashions changing over time; but I noticed they hadn't changed much.

The four of us were amongst the first in the basement and got ourselves a corner so we had walls to lean on as well as places to lie down. There was plenty of chat and movement as people settled; all against the backdrop of the wailing sirens. Some people got their heads down immediately to try to sleep, but we were all wide awake from the film and the run to the shelter.

'It was a really good film, wasn't it!' Edith said, 'I haven't enjoyed a film so much for ages.'

I nodded, 'The husband was a nasty piece of work, alright. Is anyone really that bad?' I stopped myself. If my dad had been inclined to play those sort of mind games with mum, he'd have been just as bad. In fact, he sometimes did try to convince her she was wrong about things when she was right. Luckily she was strong enough to see through him and as I got older, I could back her up.

'I'm going to say something serious now,' Bronwyn started, one of her favourite Welsh expressions, 'That woman would have had to be soft in the head to be taken in like that. I got right fed up with her. What it is, she should have trusted her own judgement more.'

Marion went very still and her eyes glistened, 'We can all be taken in by a bloke. Do you mean you never have?' she looked at Bronwyn.

Bronwyn went a bit pink, something I'd never seen before, 'Well, maybe you're right. Us women can be a bit soft in the head, like.'

A baby started crying nearby and Marion looked towards it then burst into tears. We all looked at her in amazement, it was so out of the blue. Or perhaps it wasn't.

She wiped her eyes and blew her nose. 'If I tell you all a secret, do you promise not to tell a soul?'

We all nodded.

Marion took a deep breath, 'I'm in a terrible pickle. I'm up the duff.' She began sobbing again.

Edith and Bronwyn looked at each other; stunned. I pretended I didn't already know.

Edith put her arm round Marion, 'You mean you're in the club? How many months?'

'I've missed two monthlies.'

I frowned, 'But you said at Ruth's the other day that you were having your monthly.'

'I know, I'm sorry I lied, but I couldn't tell you the truth there. Anyway, I keep hoping I'm imagining it.'

I looked around to make sure no-one could overhear us. 'Do you have any other symptoms?'

She bit her lips, 'I don't know what they are, but my bosom is a bit sore. I haven't been sick though. You always get sick in the mornings if you're in the family way, don't you? I keep hoping I'm wrong.'

'Not always,' Bronwyn said, 'I've seen my mother go through it more times than I want to remember. Sometimes she was always sick, other times she never was. Couldn't tell you why though.'

Marion put her head in her hands and sobbed again, 'What am I going to do? My dad'll thrown me out and mum won't stop him.'

'What about your boyfriend? Won't he marry you?' Bron asked.

'I thought he would. I thought we would be together forever. Shows I can be as stupid as that woman in the film. First thing he said when I told him was "Are you sure it's mine?" What does he think I am, a tart or something? He was the only one I... well, you know. I've never seen him since. I've written to him at his barracks, but he hasn't written back. I may as well be dead for all he cares.'

'What a rotter! What an absolute rotter!' Edith said.

Before we could say more someone in charge said, 'Lights out now, let's get some sleep before the All Clear.'

'We'll talk about it again in the morning,' I promised.

But the All Clear sounded a couple of hours later. Bronwyn and Edith decided to stay where they were for the night, but Marion was insistent she wanted to go home. She was still upset, and I didn't feel right letting her go on her own so I offered to go with her.

'I'll go back to our rooms after,' I told Bronwyn, 'the buses'll be running by then.'

It was a mild night, with enough light from the moon to help us on our way. It reflected off the white paint on the lamp-posts, trees and kerb edges.

Coming out of the basement it took our eyes a minute to adjust, and we stepped off the pavement and almost got run down by a man on a bicycle. Needless to say, he had no lights on it, but that didn't stop him cursing us something rotten.

London is never quiet, even in the middle of the night, in the middle of a black-out. We heard the clip-clop of a horse's hooves before we saw the horse and cart coming round the corner. The horse dropped its business right in front of us, causing a nasty smell. ARP fire fighters hurried here and there putting out small fires caused by incendiary bombs. Two men on a roof frantically tried to stop the fire spreading to nearby houses, calling instructions to each other. A drunk was singing *As you wish upon a star* as he wove his crooked way along the road.

It was too early for buses, so we continued to walk. 'Have you had any ideas what you'll do about the baby?' I asked.

There was a long pause, but I could just hear Marion gulping back tears. 'I suppose I'll have to get rid of it. Do you know any women who... you know... do that sort of thing?'

I stopped and faced her, holding her arms with my hands, 'It's not up to me to tell you what to do, but I can tell you that's so dangerous, not to mention illegal. You could die or end up in prison.'

'But I...'

We paused until the drunk went past us, having blown us loud, wet, kisses. 'My friend went to one of those women and she nearly died. It was dreadful. I was with her and I had to take her to a hospital. We were lucky the doctor didn't report her, or she'd have gone to prison.'

Marion shook herself free of my hold, 'What did they do to her?'

I remembered the awful day. We went to the abortionist's rooms. They were poor, but clean, and she was brisk and businesslike, but not unkind. I remember the smell of disinfectant, of boiled cabbage from one of the other flats on that floor and cigarette smoke. I remembered her rag rug, made of many colours. And I remembered the newspapers she put on the bed to catch the blood that ran out from my friend.

'So, what did she do to her?'

I sighed, 'I can't actually tell you, because the woman told me to hold my friend's hand and look away. I was so terrified that's what I did. I didn't dare look. I never saw what she used, but some people say it's a long piece of metal like a straightened coat hanger. You can see how easily it could go wrong.'

She held my hand, 'I've tried everything I can think of. I've drunk gin, I've had scalding hot baths, and I've jumped up and down until I was fair worn out. I don't know what else to try.'

An ambulance went by, ringing its bell, and we had to wait to speak again.

'I went round his house, you know. Or where he told me

he lived. We never went in there because he said his mum was against him having a girlfriend. But he pointed it out to me once from a bus because I'd asked him a few times where he lived.'

The sky was gradually lightning as dawn approached and we could hear the birds singing even over all the wartime noise. I thought it was amazing they stayed somewhere so dangerous.

I turned off my torch, 'That was brave, Marion. What did he say?'

'Nothing. He couldn't, could he, because he didn't even live there. He'd never lived there. It was another one of his lies. See, I think if I go to his Commanding Officer nothing will come of it. They can tell him what to do all they like, but he'll never do it. He'll just go AWOL or something.'

I put my arm through hers again, 'What an absolute stinker he is. And to take advantage of you like that,' she got her hanky out again and blew her nose. 'You are in a pickle, Marion, but promise me you won't do anything dangerous. Let's talk about it again in a day or two and see if we can think of something.'

CHAPTER 8

𝒶s always the station was busy; soldiers with kitbags over their shoulders; travellers lugging suitcases; mothers clinging on to wayward children - all hoping the train they wanted would arrive on time. Unintelligible station announcements, and the general hubbub made conversation difficult.

'Are you sure you want to go?' I said, my mouth close to Marion's ear. She knew I was talking about the mother-and-baby home.

She got out her purse to pay for the train tickets, 'I don't think I have much choice. My bump will show soon, and we know what my dad'll will do then. And I think mum has noticed I've missed my monthlies.'

A woman behind us looked interested in what we were saying, and so we stopped speaking for a while.

We eventually got to the front of the line, 'Two third class tickets to Colchester, please.' Marion handed the money over and took our tickets.

'I really want to pay for my own ticket,' I said.

She gave a sad smile, 'It's the least I can do when you're kind enough to give up your day off to come with me.'

The train was far too packed to continue our conversation. We tried to talk about everyday things or to join in conversations in our carriage, but Marion's mind was a million miles away. I held her hand a couple of times when she looked on the verge of tears.

The journey took ages. As usual there were stops for no apparent reasons, but it was pleasant when we left London behind and began travelling through the Essex countryside. We tried to identify the crops growing in the fields, but Townies that we were, we had no idea what most of them were. Land Girls stopped work to wave at the train and we waved back, envying their work in the fresh air. School boys who were helping them to earn some pocket money, more often pulled silly faces, and two even flashed their bums, laughing their heads off.

What seemed like hours later, we pulled into Colchester station. It's an army barracks town so loads of soldiers got off with us and another lot waited to get on. I dug an old map of the town out of my bag and decided we could walk to the mother-and-baby home, St. Mungo's Hostel. Army vehicles were everywhere, and soldiers marched along the main road reminding me of my initial training when I never thought I'd learn which way to turn.

As we walked up the hill, we noticed the houses and other buildings were intact. We were so used to seeing bomb sites that an undamaged town seemed odd.

'Well, if you come here, you won't have to worry about bombs,' I said, hoping to cheer her up, 'I heard they only had one night of bombing and that was a couple of years ago. Flattened a hospital, I read somewhere.'

We'd heard some horror stories about mother-and-baby

homes. Girls treated like slaves; not allowed to even use their own names; babies 'sold' to make money for convents that pretended to act in a Christian way; babies removed even after the girls decided to keep them. This one was supposed to be okay, but that didn't stop me having butterflies in my tummy as we walked towards, it even though we were just visiting. I could barely imagine how Marion felt.

The home was in a big double fronted house behind a brick wall with overhanging trees. Pregnant girls were tidying the front garden, well hidden from the road. A nun walked around like a head teacher, her hands behind her back, checking that they were working as they should be.

Army vehicles rumbled outside, contrasting with the clip-clip of a horse and cart. A boy ran behind the horse, panting to keep up. He had a bucket and shovel and was scooping up the horse droppings to sell for manure.

As we walked towards the door, the nun looked at us and nodded but said nothing. When her back was turned briefly, one of the girls looked at us, shook her head, then quickly looked back to what she was doing.

The front door was massive, as you'd expect with a big property. It was dark wood, with a shining door knocker and letter box, no doubt cleaned by the expectant mothers. Dents and scratches, polished so well you could hardly see them, showed life had not always been peaceful in the building.

We knocked on the door, and it was opened so quickly the nun must have been waiting just inside.

'We've come to see Mother Superior,' Marion said, her voice trembling.

The nun walked ahead of us, her long habit swishing as she moved. We were taken along a corridor that smelled of polish and faintly, of vegetables cooking. A baby cried in the distance and I saw Marion tense.

'Here we are,' the nun said and knocked on the last door on the right. Mother Superior looked up with a smile as we were shown in. Her office was at the back of the building overlooking a spacious garden.

'Marion?' she looked from one to the other of us, unsure who was who. Within weeks there would be no mistaking.

'It's me,' Marion said, stepping forward.

'Well, sit down, Girls.' she stood and turned to a table behind her, 'Would you like a glass of water? I imagine you must be thirsty after your journey.'

'Now, Marion,' she said, once she'd handed us both glasses. She tucked her hands inside the wide sleeves of her habit, 'When is your baby due?'

Marion looked down at her hands folded in her lap, 'About another five months, I think. I'm not really sure.'

'So you haven't consulted a doctor yet?'

Marion shook her head, 'It's... it's... so embarrassing. And it costs money.'

Mother Superior shuffled some papers on her desk, 'Do your family not belong to a club to help save for medical costs?'

'No, there's never enough to spare. We just get by.'

'I see. Well, that might be a problem, but we can probably find a way round it. Now, why don't you go round the home with Sister Agatha. She'll be able to answer any questions you may have.'

She rang a brass bell on her desk and the door opened immediately.

'Sister Agatha, can you show Marion and her friend round, please?'

The sister nodded, 'Come with me.'

We followed her up a lovely staircase with mahogany handrails. It had a turn before the top, and a beautiful stained glass window depicting Jesus healing the sick threw bright colours over the woodwork. There were two bathrooms which were old fashioned with some enamel missing on the bath, but spotlessly clean.

'We expect our girls to earn their keep while they're here,' Sister Agatha said, 'there is a rota of household chores and cleaning. We believe that cleanliness is next to Godliness. And the work often teaches the girls housewifely skills they may not otherwise know. They'll be very useful for them later in life.'

The bedrooms, more like dormitories really, were separated between those for girls who had not had their babies yet, and those who had. The rooms were empty, with the beds made immaculately. It was very impersonal with only bibles on each bedside table. A large cross was on the wall opposite the window. I wondered where the girls kept their belongings as there only seemed to be a small cupboard between the beds for storage.

The rooms for the girls who'd had their babies showed no sign of baby equipment.

'Girls like you,' Sister Agatha said, in a tone that hinted at criticism, 'find the friendship of others who are in the same situation of comfort. And seeing so much unhappiness should be a lesson to avoid any immoral behaviour in the future. Luckily, God forgives transgressions as long as we repent. Repentance is something you'll have time to think about while you're here.'

Marion and I looked at each other, jaws tight.

'This is a good time to tell you that we march to St Jude's Church every Sunday...'

'You mean everyone sees us?' Marion said, speaking for the first time.

'That is correct. Then every evening we have a half hour service before our evening meal. What religion are you?'

'Church of England, but...'

'You'll be fine then, this is a Church of England convent. Now, let me show you the baby room.'

I held Marion's hand as we walked behind the nun. She led us to a large room overlooking the front garden and street. Like the others, it had a high ceiling and was light and airy. Two long windows let in sunshine and dust motes danced slowly in the sunbeams. The babies were lined up in rectangular cribs with the name of each child on a label at one end. There were eight babies in all, and four empty cribs.

One baby was restless, whimpering in her sleep; the others slept peacefully.

'One of our girls, Barbara, is feeding her child in the next room. We allow girls to come for six weeks before the birth, and six weeks after. It gives them time to bond with their child if they decide to keep it, but most choose to have their baby adopted.'

I'd read about that. It was also time to check that the baby had no disabilities. Adoptive parents wanted perfect babies.

While Marion was talking to Sister Agatha, I looked out of the window. Through the trees I could see a car parked directly outside. Through an open window, I heard the front door open and saw a couple walk out holding a baby wrapped in a white knitted shawl. 'I hope you'll be very happy with him,' Mother Superior said.

I looked down at the garden. A girl came from the side of the house, saw what was happening, and stopped as suddenly as if she'd walked into a wall. Her hands went over her mouth and she doubled up, sobbing. The couple with the baby began to turn to see what the noise was, but Mother Superior hurried them out to their car.

One of the other girls went over and tried to comfort the sobbing girl, but the supervising nun pulled her away and told the young mother to get back into the house. It was all I could do to hold back tears as I watched the tragedy unfold. If Marion came here or somewhere similar, she would have to give up the child she'd learned to love. But what choice did she have?

Looking at the scene I tried to decide if the nuns had been unkind. While it looked like it, perhaps they tried to make the sadness of the moment as brief as possible. I guessed that the young mother was not supposed to see her baby being taken by its new parents - poor thing.

I turned back as Marion and Sister Agnes were about to leave the room. Marion was wiping her eyes. 'You said I could only come six weeks before the baby is due, but I'll show before then and I'll have nowhere to live!'

One of the babies started crying and Sister Agnes guided Marion down the corridor and back downstairs. 'We often get girls in your position,' she said, 'we have an arrangement with a guest house in town. They will put you up and feed you in return for you working there.'

Marion blew her nose, 'What sort of work?'

'General cleaning, changing the beds - that sort of thing, what you'd expect from a guest house.'

She led the way to the kitchen. It was large with flagstones and an ancient Aga type cooker. A massive wooden table stood in the middle. On it was a basket of vegetables; several loaves of bread and various piles of crockery. Three pregnant girls were preparing a meal, guided by another nun.

'I explained we have a rota,' Sister Agnes said, 'that includes cooking. You'd be amazed how many girls don't have the first idea how to prepare a nutritious meal. Even with rationing, good food is possible. And talking of that, we would need your ration book, of course. Can you cook?'

Marion went pink in the face, 'My mum does the cooking in our house.'

Sister Agatha frowned, 'Well, we like to think our girls go home with more skills than when they arrived. I'm sure the good Lord would approve of that.'

An elderly man with a bent back was mowing the back lawn. It was tiny because most of the space had been turned into a vegetable plot. But there was space immediately next to the house to sit and prepare those vegetables and get a bit of fresh air.

We went back to Mother Superior's room when we'd finished the tour, but when Sister Agatha knocked, there was no answer. Mother Superior had gone out.

'I expect I've answered all your questions,' the nun said, 'and you can always phone or write if you think of anything else.'

Marion hitched her gas mask higher on her shoulder, 'I'd like the address of the guest house you talked about, please.'

'It's Blue View Guest House on Walton Road. Do you think you can remember that? It's quite close to the town centre - the other side.'

We said our goodbyes, and stepped back onto the pavement. Imagine my surprise when a voice said, 'Hello, Lily, didn't expect to see you...'

The speaker looked at my face, looked at the building we'd just left, then looked at my stomach.

It took me a minute to recognise the man in army uniform, 'It's Gordon, isn't it?'

'That's right. I'm one of Edward's friends. We met when I bumped into you last time he was home on leave. Is all well with you?'

I felt I was putting myself and Marion in a difficult situation. 'I'm well, thank you, but please excuse us if we push on. We have an appointment.'

He saluted and smiled, 'Are you sure I can't buy you and your friend some refreshments? I have the time.'

'I'm so sorry,' I said, secretly relieved not to have time to take up his offer, 'we have to be somewhere.'

He shrugged his shoulders, 'Okay, that's a pity, but I'll be sure to let Edward know I've seen you.'

As we walked away Marion grinned, 'You know he thinks it's you that's in the family way.'

'Surely not. Why would he even know what that building is for?'

'Are you serious? Word spreads about things like that.'

'What did you think of the Home?' I asked.

'St Mungo's?' she paused, 'I worried when that girl shook her head as we walked in, but it didn't seem too bad. Not when you consider all the horror stories we hear.'

'It was a bit sort of, clinical, I thought,' I said, 'not much warmth from the nuns.'

She laughed, 'There's not much warmth at all at home, so I'll be used to that. Well, Mum's not bad but she lets Dad tell her what to do. At least I'll have the other girls to talk to and no men trying to take advantage of me.'

I stopped walking and turned to her, 'Does that happen at home?'

She looked away, 'It's not something I want to talk about.'

My mum's ex-boyfriend had tried to get fresh with me, but at least I wasn't living at home at the time so I could get away. If Marion had to put up with that in the only place she had to live, that would be just awful. I changed the subject.

'The Home was nice and clean, and you'd get well fed. That's something.'

She put her hand on her stomach, 'But I'd still have to give my baby away. I try not to, but I keep thinking how lovely it would be if I could keep it. My very own child; someone to love who would love me. I've even started to think of names. Silly, I know, but I can't help it.'

I held her hand, 'I don't think it's silly at all. I bet all girls do that. And from what I've read, you'll register the baby's birth, so you'll need names.'

She nodded, 'The new people...' she paused and gulped, 'the new mum and dad will probably change whatever name I choose.'

'But you'll choose it with love and who knows, one day when your little one is grown up you might find each other,' I paused, 'I meant to ask if you ever heard anything from the father's Commanding Officer?'

'No. Nothing. I bet this happens a lot. Makes me wonder if the top brass don't want to know, or want to keep it hush-hush.'

We passed the Army Garrison. It wasn't the one where her ex-boyfriend was stationed, but that didn't stop her looking round. Some new recruits were practicing marching, many of them forgetting which was their right leg or left. The Sergeant Major was shouting abuse at them, just like mine did to me. Other squaddies were hurrying round carrying big wooden boxes, although we couldn't tell what they contained. They could have been guns or tinned spam for all we knew. There were long rows of wooden huts, almost certainly their dormitories, and nearer the entrance gates some square brick buildings which must have been the offices.

Although all the men were busy, we still got a few wolf-whistles. Marion gave a sad smile, 'I won't be getting any of them soon.'

'You will again though.' I said, trying not to think about the heart-ache she faced.

We walked down to the city centre and found the British Restaurant which was set up in a church hall. Union Jack bunting was strung across the ceiling, and a big crucifix was on one wall. There was a raised stage with red curtains pulled back. 'Thank goodness for these places,' I said as we waited to go in, 'most meals sixpence and you don't need a ration book.'

The tables and chairs were a crazy mixture of anything they could find and some were quite rickety. But every single table was covered in matching American cloth which was easy to wipe down.

'Even at those prices my family couldn't afford to eat here.' Marion said, 'this is a treat for me.'

'Well, don't have the fish; I heard it's not great. But the fishcakes are okay.'

She wrinkled her nose, 'I've never had fish unless it's fish and chips from the chippie on the corner.'

She looked at the menu, 'I think I'll play safe and have mince and mash. Oh, and they've got spotted dick and custard. Yummy!'

We changed our pennies for tokens; different colours for each course. But they never came to more than ten pence for the lot. The Women's Voluntary Service women who ran the place looked very smart in their green uniforms. They kept a tight ship too - you'd think they were in the army. I half expected to be put on a charge if I dropped anything.

Once we'd got our meal we looked around at the other people in the restaurant. To my surprise there were not many people in uniform; I supposed they'd get their meals on the base. There were some very well dressed ladies who I guessed might be on duty in the restaurant sometimes. Other than that, we were a mixed bunch; women looking tired after a morning queuing for food; workers in their dinner break and a few retired people.

We ate without talking much, and left feeling absolutely stuffed.

~

Blue View Guest House was strangely named; not being near the sea or even the River Colne. It was a detached, double fronted house, but there the similarity to St Mungo's ended. The walls were painted a duck egg blue and the door and window frames were white. There were two sash windows either side of the door, and three upstairs although the middle one was strangely off-centre. Heavy lace curtains covered all the windows which also showed the taped crosses against bomb blasts.

Most of the houses in the street were semi-detached with bay windows; their front gardens well tended. It was a busy street with plenty of traffic.

We hadn't made an appointment so we knocked on the front door without much hope. A painfully thin young girl with dreadful acne answered. She wore a traditional maid's outfit; a black dress with a white Peter Pan collar and a white frilly apron over the top. Her stomach pushed her apron forward. Her skin was darkish; much like Bronwyn's with the same crinkly hair. I wondered if her parents were different colours like Bronwyn's.

'Can I help you, me Duck?' she said in a broad London accent.

'Can we see Mrs...' we realised we hadn't asked the name of the lady we should contact. 'Mrs...'

'Is it the lady of the house you wanna see? Mrs Thompson?'

As she spoke a tall woman came from the back of the house, a frown on her brow, 'Who is it, Bella?'

Bella's dark skin paled, and she clasped the edge of her apron. 'I don't know Mrs Thompson, they only just...'

'Get back to the cleaning!' Mrs Thompson ordered without looking at her, 'I'll be along to check on your work in a minute, so make sure it's done properly.'

'You can't trust these Darkies, can you?' she said, assuming we'd agree.

I clenched my jaw; better not argue with her in case it affected Marion's chances of getting a place there.

'We've just been to St Mungo's,' she said, 'they suggested we come here because...'

Mrs Thompson looked at Marion's stomach, folded her arms and took a deep breath, 'Let me guess, you're in the family way. Not very far gone yet from the look of you,' she stepped back and indicated the hallway with her hand, 'You'd better come in, I suppose. You and your friend.'

We stepped into the hallway, off which was a staircase in the centre. At the top there were landings in both directions. The house smelled of polish and baking. 'We do all our own cooking here, bread and everything. So much better than the awful stuff from the bakers'. I have my own contacts, you know, to get flour and other essentials. So important to maintain standards. Come through to the kitchen.'

The kitchen was smaller than expected for the size of the house and very dated. A girl, well along judging by the size of her, was peeling potatoes and another was chopping cabbage. They both tensed as we walked in, but didn't look up.

'I have up to four girls in your position,' Mrs Thompson

said, running her finger along a skirting board, checking for dust, 'and there are five paying guests. Mostly long-termers, of course,' she sniffed, 'people like staying here. I live in the two back rooms.'

'Would I...' Marion began.

'Would you what? Have to work? Get paid? Have your boyfriend in? I've been asked all these things. Yes, you have to work, that's in return for your keep - board and lodgings. No, you can't have your boyfriend here, although I suspect he did a runner like most of them or you probably wouldn't be here. You get a half day off a week and you get paid one pound a week. And I'll need your ration book, of course.'

Marion gripped my hand, 'Perhaps you could show us round,' she said, her voice little more than a whisper.

Just then the doorbell rang. A minute later Bella came into the kitchen, 'Someone to see you, Mrs Thompson. A gentleman looking for a room for a week.'

Mrs Thompson straightened her back and turned to the girl peeling potatoes, 'Cathy, show these girls around. Not in the private rooms of course! I'll be back soon.'

When she'd gone, Cathy dried her hands on a tea towel. They were red raw, her nails bitten to the quick. She took off her flowery wrap-around pinny. It was so well worn you could almost see through it. I wondered how many girls in her position had used it. 'You'd better come with me then,' she said, 'we'll go to our bedrooms first. They're in the attic.'

As we climbed up the stairs, we could hear Mrs Thompson talking to her potential customer. Her voice was really posh.

Everywhere was spotless; the windows shone between their tapes; the skirting boards and picture frames were dust free; and a healthy aspidistra stood on the landing in a huge china pot. Its leaves shone so much they must have been polished.

Cathy didn't say a word until we got to the attic floor. There were four narrow beds in the long room, each with beds made up perfectly. I would have expected a teddy bear or some other personal things, but there was nothing. There were two dormer windows facing the back of the house. It was a clean but cheerless room with little sign that it was occupied.

She turned to Marion, 'You good at cleaning?' she asked.

'I suppose so, I help my mum.'

Cathy closed the door, then turned to us, her face grim, 'Look, I'm gonna tell you what this place is like. But before I say a word, you've gotta promise not to repeat a word I'm saying or Mrs Hitler will throw me out.'

'I promise,' Marion whispered.

'Me too.'

'Just look around this place,' she swept her arm around indicating the room, 'does it look like she gives a stuff about us? She has us working all hours God sends. Up at five and never stop to draw breath 'til bedtime. She don't give a hoot how far on you are,' she put her hands on her swollen stomach. 'We get half an hour in the middle of the day to eat a sandwich - never what the paying guests are getting, mind you. Oh no, leftovers are good enough for us! And if she finds anything wrong, and she always does, she docks money out of our pay. No-one has ever had a pound yet, that's for sure. She's a bit handy too.' She mimed someone being smacked round the head.

Marion looked like she might pass out, and I grabbed her arm to steady her, 'Oh dear,' she said, her voice shaky, 'I don't think I have any other choice but here.'

Cathy looked at her stomach, 'Looks like you've got a

little while to find somewhere. Don't come here unless you're desperate - really desperate.'

'Are you girls all right up there?' Mrs Thompson called from downstairs, 'the cooking needs attention.'

We opened the door and Cathy put her hands to her lips. We nodded; we wouldn't say a word.

'Thank you for showing us round,' I said loud enough for Mrs Thompson to hear.

We went back down to the entrance hall and Cathy headed to the kitchen without a word. 'How did you get on then?' Mrs Thompson asked, her voice bright and chirpy.

'It was very interesting, thank you for showing us round. We'll let you know a bit nearer the time.' I looked at my watch, 'I'm so sorry, but we'd better hurry or we'll miss our train home.'

The weather had changed in the short time we were in there. The wind had come up and trees on the street were blowing around as if they wanted to escape the ground. Empty ciggie packets and bits of paper blew down the street racing to get to the corner first. We hurried along, holding on to our hats, but got no further than the end of the road when it started to rain; huge drops as big as a man's thumb nail. We ducked into a shop doorway, luckily it was closed; it must have been half-day closing.

We shook our hats and brushed the water off our shoulders. 'What did you think of that place, Marion?' I asked, 'could you stand it? She seemed a bit of a monster to me.'

Her bottom lip trembled, 'If there's nothing else I can do, I suppose I'll have to go there. It sounds bloody awful though - excuse my swearing. It's plain not fair. You go with a bloke 'cos you think he loves you and he'll marry you. Then he gets you up the duff and just walks away. Leaves us girls to deal with everything. It's just not fair.'

'No, it's not fair. Never was and never will be.'

An army lorry went by, the back covered with canvas. Two soldiers hung out of the flap at the back, indifferent to the rain. 'Want a lift, Sweetheart?' they shouted.

'Only if you're going to the station!' I shouted back, but by then they were too far away to hear me.

We waited twenty minutes in that shop doorway for the rain to pass. Mostly we were silent, thinking through what we'd seen that day.

Would Marion really have to subject herself to life under Mrs Hitler?

CHAPTER 9

'*H*ow are you getting on driving ambulances?' I asked Bronwyn. We were both home on the same evening, a rare event.

She finished washing a plate and handed it to me to dry, 'The driving's easy. I loved riding the bike, but with all the problems on the roads from the bombing I suppose it was an accident waiting to happen. But I wish The Red Cross had given us more first aid training. Some of the things we have to deal with!' she stopped herself, 'but you'd know all about that, Cariad, you've been dealing with them for ages.'

I put the plate on our wonky kitchen table, 'You're not kidding. It's like we see horrendous things at least once a week. Not to mentioned dealing with people who call us puffed up Hitlers because we tell them to cover their lights.'

Bronwyn raised an eyebrow, 'I backed into a fence yesterday, smashed it to bits, didn't see it at all in the dark. Luckily the house had already been bombed, although strange that bits of the fence were still there, but weird things happen every day in the bombing. The other drivers will never let me forget it. We give each other hell, but it's all in good fun.'

'You thrown up yet when you've seen something awful?' I asked.

'Twice,' she said, 'what about you?'

'Three times, but often I have to do some deep breathing to carry on. We're supposed to be professionals even if we are volunteers, but we're human too.'

We finished the dishes and made a pot of tea, 'I'm looking forward to reading my book, then there's that new play on the wireless.'

Bronwyn groaned, 'I suppose I'd better write to my mam. Not that she ever writes back even though I send her some money sometimes. Swansea's had a lot of bombing. For all I know, the whole lot of them could be dead.' She went over to one of the cardboard boxes that made up some of our furniture and took out a sheet of paper and an envelope.

I sat down on one of our two armchairs, my tea in my hand, 'Will you tell her about the ambulance work?'

She tapped her teeth with her pencil, 'Tell you the truth, I'm in two minds. I'll probably leave out the gory details. Life's hard enough for her as it is.'

I took a sip of my tea, 'Before you start writing, there's something I want to ask you.'

She looked up, relieved to delay letter writing, 'What's that then?'

'You know Marion's going to get chucked out by her dad soon. How about letting her stay here? We can get three mattresses in our bedroom okay, and we get on with her.'

Bronwyn sat back in her chair, silent for a few seconds, 'I don't see as how we can have a baby here. We'd get our marching orders double quick!'

I shook my head, 'I didn't mean that. She's planning to have the baby adopted. She can go to the mother-and-baby home six weeks before the baby's due. I meant between now and then. It would save her going to that awful guest house I told you about. She'd be so badly treated there, and she doesn't deserve that.'

Before Bronwyn could answer we heard loud voices from upstairs. 'You did what! You stupid woman!' we heard Thomas shout. We couldn't hear Wendy reply, but then we heard a chair clatter to the floor: a bang; then silence.

'Do you think that's Wendy bouncing off the wall? Or the floor? I know that sound; heard it often enough when my dad was around and in a chopsing mood.'

My heart raced and I bit my lip, 'What if she's dead? We should go and get the police.'

She laughed, 'Where? There's none close to here. They wouldn't do anything anyway. As far as the cops are concerned men are allowed to beat the living daylights out of their wives. Half of them probably do it as well.'

We crept into the hall, keeping absolutely quiet, and listened. A couple of minutes later we heard the chair being banged again, if it was a chair. It sounded like Thomas was putting it upright.

'DO YOU UNDERSTAND NOW? DO I HAVE TO TELL YOU AGAIN?'

We heard a dragging sound, 'Do you think that's him dragging her along the floor?' I whispered.

'Could be her dragging herself out of his way. I've seen my mam do that lots of times.' Bronwyn's eyes were hard as steel, 'I honestly don't know why we bother with bloody men.'

We waited a few more minutes but there was no more sound. Then, ten minutes later as we settled in our armchairs we heard the unmistakable sound of the springs on their bed bouncing.

'Some sort of making it up!' Bronwyn growled.

CHAPTER 10

 he sun shone as we headed out of the Depot to eat our sandwiches. Finding a green space got harder and harder because although we weren't being bombed so often, unsafe houses were being demolished and a lot of parks turned into allotments. Marion, Bronwyn and I decided to explore a route we hadn't taken before. It was along a busy road with lots of shops, offices and traffic, but we thought we could find somewhere to sit at the edge of an allotment at the far end. It was a mild day, and I looked up at the sky hoping the rain would hold off until we got back to the Depot.

We walked past the endless queues of women trying to find enough food to feed their family. It seemed like the lines got longer every day, and often when you got to the end of it, there was little or no choice of meat or fish or whatever you wanted. 'Thank goodness we can afford to go to the British Restaurant sometimes,' I said as I looked at them.

'What are you waiting for?' Marion asked the woman at the end of one queue.

She shrugged her shoulders, 'No idea, but I hope it's something good!'

We'd all bought our pack of sandwiches and a bottle of water. The allotment was nearer than we thought and we were glad there was a strip of grass along one side where we could sit. Posters around the wire fence told us to 'Save kitchen scraps to feed to the hens' and 'Make do and mend' and 'Lend five shillings to your country and crush the Germans.'

'How is your place coming on? Have you sorted out the garden yet?' Marion asked, unwrapping her food.

Bronwyn and I looked at each other. It turned out she could be a demon at scrubbing floors, but was absolutely useless in the garden, 'Never had one, see, wouldn't know what to do with one!' she had moaned when I tried to get her interested.

'I've cleared about a quarter of it,' I said. 'I need to find out what veg will grow if I plant them this time of year.'

'Can't help you there,' Marion said, 'what's in your sandwiches?'

'Fish paste as usual, but some tomato as well.' I said.

'Stale cheese and tomato,' Bronwyn said.

We ended up sharing them.

'Gotta ask,' Bronwyn said, 'did you ever hear from that lump of a boyfriend of yours?'

Marion's face fell, 'I got one letter,' she patted her stomach, 'he told me to get rid of it. And he said it probably wasn't his anyway. How could he be so cruel? He knew he was the love of my life. I cried myself to sleep for a week.'

My jaw dropped open, 'I don't usually swear, but that man, no that boy, is a bastard. Although he's left you in the lurch, at least you're not stuck with him for life. When this is all over you'll find someone good. Plenty more fish in the sea and all that. Have your mum and dad realised you're in the family way yet?'

Marion took a deep breath, the corners of her mouth

turned down, 'Mum keeps giving me funny looks, I'm sure she's guessed. My dad is mostly either at work or asleep in the armchair. Lucky he doesn't really look at me much. But I can't do up my skirts now, I have to use a safety pin and soon that won't be enough. I'm going to have to go to that bed and breakfast in Colchester.'

I looked at Bronwyn and she gave me a little nod, 'How would you feel about coming and staying with us until you go to St Mungo's?'

She went still then looked from one of us to the other, 'Are you joking? You'd do that? What about the neighbours looking down on me?'

Bronwyn laughed, 'It's like this, see. We gets you a ring from Woolworth's, and hey presto, you're an army wife. Hubby is away doing his bit for Britain. You've been bombed out and you're staying with us until you find somewhere new. Loads of people are staying with friends after they're bombed out. No-one will think it's weird.'

Marion started to cry with big sobs that made her chest heave, 'Oh, Bronwyn, Lily, I'll never be able to thank you enough. It's like a dream come true.'

'Before you thank us,' I said with a laugh, 'you'll have to buy yourself a bed!'

She was so happy as we walked back to the Depot she almost had a skip in her step. Then something happened to instantly snatch away her happiness. The Registrar's office was on the High Street in the middle of the shops. A single story building, it nonetheless had an imposing look with Greek columns either side of the door. It stood back from the shops, with two steps down to a flat area in front for cars or for newlyweds to have their photos taken.

We were on the opposite side of the street, and not taking

much notice until a small group of people came out of the building and started to laugh and cheer.

'Let's wait a minute,' Marion said, 'I always like a wedding.'

She was to regret those words.

The new happy couple stood on top of the steps smiling. The man was in uniform and the woman was in a smart blue suit and a little box hat.

The groom was Marion's ex-boyfriend.

A car near us backfired and he glanced over. He spotted Marion, locked eyes with her briefly, then looked away as if she didn't exist. A glimpse of a sneer moved his lips.

Marion held her breath for so long I thought she'd faint. Then she let out a long breath and stamped her foot.

'I'm not going to cry! I won't give him the satisfaction!' Her voice had real determination. She walked away so quickly we almost had to run to keep up with her.

Under her breath I could hear her swearing repeatedly, 'Bloody son of a bitch. Bastard!' He was lucky she didn't cross the road to tell his new wife what a rat she'd just married.

I stopped her before we got to the Depot. 'Marion, perhaps you should have the afternoon off to calm down. I'll tell Mr Lynch you're sick.'

'She's right,' Bronwyn said, 'you'll never concentrate, Cariad.'

She looked at us, tears streaming down her face, then she nodded and turned around, walking slowly in the opposite direction.

'I'll come to see you later!' I called after her.

∼

I was later than I intended getting to her house. An air raid alarm went off as I was on my way there, but it wasn't long before the All Clear sounded. Marion lived in a narrow street of terraced houses, many of which were poorly cared for, although others showed them up with dazzling white doorsteps and polished brass door furniture. Her home was one of these.

I knocked on the door, uncertain what I would find. Marion may have decided to tell her mum and dad about the baby or about her boyfriend getting married. I'd have to tread carefully not to put my foot in it.

The door was opened by her dad who looked surprised to see me there. He nodded and pushed past me without a word. He looked as if he'd just had a wash; his hair was wet and stuck to his head as if it was painted on. When he'd gone, I was left not knowing what to do. The door was open, so I took one step inside. The walls were painted a yellowy cream and there were three flying plaster ducks on the right. A green patterned rug covered the most worn part of the Lino on the floor. The house smelled of baking and made my mouth water. I shouted for Marion. A minute later her mum appeared from the kitchen.

'You one of Marion's friends?' she asked, wiping her hands on her pinny.

'Yes, I'm Lily and we work together at the Depot. Is she in?'

She nodded, 'Yes, she came home early from work, wasn't feeling well. I haven't heard a peek out of her since.'

She went to the bottom of the stairs, 'MARION, someone to see you,' she turned to me, 'What did you say your name was?'

'It's Lily.'

'IT'S LILY. LILY'S COME TO SEE YOU.'

We heard noises upstairs and Marion came to the top of the stairs. 'Can you come up, Lily? I'm still not feeling well.'

I looked at her mum to see if it was okay. 'Go on up,' she said, 'I'll bring you both a cuppa in a mo.'

Lily had the small box room on the side of the house. A narrow single bed was pushed against the wall and a wooden chair served as a bedside table. Her clothes were in the smallest wardrobe I'd ever seen. Until all this happened Marion had always been outgoing and a bit of a racy dresser. It was hard to match that up with this very warm but conservative home.

She sat on the bed and patted the cover for me to sit next to her. Her face was blotchy and her usually immaculate hair was a bird's nest.

'I'm going to tell Mum,' she said, her voice shaking.

I frowned, 'I'm confused, what will you tell her? About the baby or your boyfriend getting married?'

She grabbed my arm, 'I'm going to tell her both and I'm scared to death. Will you stay while I tell her?'

I wanted to run away; anything to avoid being there while she told. 'Marion, if you tell her now and she throws you out, well, we don't have a bed for you yet, or even a mattress. Can you wait 'til tomorrow?'

She gave a bitter laugh, 'I'll sleep on the floor,' she turned to me, eyes wide with terror, 'you haven't changed your mind about letting me stay have you?'

I put my arm round her shoulders, 'No of course not. We can sort out a bed tomorrow.'

There was a tap on the door and Marion's mum came in with a tray of tea and two biscuits. 'Fresh out of the oven, these are,' she said, 'how are you feeling, Love. Any better?'

I looked at Marion and she nodded, 'I think you'd better sit down, Mrs White.' I said.

She sat down with the tray on her knee, her face tight with worry, 'What is it? Is it something serious? Shall I get the doctor?'

I took the tray off her, 'Marion has something to tell you.'

She looked at Marion who turned redder than a rose, 'It's well... Mum... please don't hate me...'

'Why on earth would I hate you? You're my little girl!'

'Mum, it's... well... I'm... I'm up the duff.'

Her mum blinked hard, frowning. 'What do you mean, you're up the duff?'

'I'm in the family way. I'm having a baby.'

Mrs White's hand went to her heart, 'Nooooooo... don't say that... please don't say that... what will the neighbours... you and that boy... I told you you can't trust him, not with those shifty eyes.' A silent scream turned her mouth into a circle. Tears rolled down her cheeks and she wiped them away with a tea towel from the tray.

Without another word she rushed from the room and we heard her lock herself in the bathroom.

Marion looked at me, 'What should I do?'

I shrugged, 'You know your mum better than me. Does she often react to things so strongly?'

She shook her head, 'She gets in a two-and-eight sometimes, but not like this. She usually just shouts.' She put her head in her hands again.

I looked round her room. It was small, but full of her personal belongings. A well-loved teddy sat on her pillow, one eye missing; a hairbrush and powder compact; a book on the chair next to her bed and on the wall was a picture of her favourite film-star, Cary Grant. Bronwyn and I had moved around so much since we joined up that we had few personal belongings, but I remembered the first time I suddenly had to leave my home. I felt lost and bewildered for ages. Marion would have to face that as well as the baby growing inside her.

We sat silently until we heard her mother come out of the bathroom. She came back into the bedroom with a determined look on her face. 'So when's he going to make an honest woman of you?'

Marion reached out to touch her mum's hand, but it was snatched away, 'You were right, Mum, he couldn't be trusted. When I told him, he didn't want to know and now he's married someone else instead. Today. That's why I came home early, Lily and me walked past the Registrar's Office and he was coming out. He totally ignored me.' She was in tears too.

'Was his new wife in the family way, too?' her mum asked.

Marion was sobbing too much to answer, so I spoke for her, 'We couldn't tell, Mrs White. If she was, it wasn't enough to show. It was a quiet wedding; only about six of them there, so I suppose it could be.'

She sniffed, 'Or it could just be war-time rations didn't stretch to a big do. I hope he rots in hell, the total bounder.'

There was silence for a minute, then Marion spoke, 'I've got a place in a mother-and-baby home for the last six weeks. Then I'll have the baby adopted. Lily and Bronwyn will let me stay with them until then.'

Mrs White's face was blotchy from crying. She rubbed the heel of her hand against her chest, 'You're giving it up? Adopted? I suppose you'll have to. My first grandchild, and I'll never know it. I've always wanted grandchildren.'

Marion looked down at her hands, 'I'm so sorry, Mum. I never thought...'

'I thought you'd put on a bit of weight. You know what'll happen when your dad finds out. He'll go crazy. He'll chuck you out sure as eggs is eggs.'

I spoke up, 'Like Marion said, me and Bronwyn have got a flat and Marion can stay with us. Trouble is, we don't have a bed for her.'

She tucked her hair behind her ears, just like Marion did and looked at me properly for the first time. 'You'd do that? You'd take her in?'

'We'd all have to share a bedroom, but it's just big enough. We'll get by. She can stay 'til she goes to the Home.'

She went quiet for a while, looking from Marion to me.

'Mum...' Marion started.

'Sshhh, I'm thinking. Let me work this out.'

She bit her thumb nail, 'Look, I know what to do. You get packed tonight. I'll tell your dad you've got food poisoning and you won't be coming downstairs. He's always gone before you get up in the morning. That way you won't have to lie to him. You can pack up the stuff you need to take, but hide it in case he comes in to see you.' she paused and bit her nail again, 'the bloke at number 23s got a van. I'll ask him to move your bed tomorrow. Your dad'll go bananas when he finds out, but you won't be here to face the music and I've had plenty of practice at dealing with him.'

She turned to me, 'Will I be able to visit Marion when she's staying with you?'

'Yes, of course. We can have visitors.' I didn't say I wasn't sure if we could have people to stay. We'd cross that bridge if we came to it.

CHAPTER 11

*R*uth was turning the letter over and over in her hands, a deep frown on her brow. 'There's something wrong. I know it,' she said.

We were the last two in the office after a busy day. It was quiet apart from the hubbub from the lorries and workmen outside. Covers were on typewriters and papers were locked away in filing cabinets. I wanted to finish a bit of work and planned to go straight to my ARP duties, so there was no point in hurrying. I'd noticed Ruth dawdling which was unlike her. Since she'd joined the WVS she usually left promptly.

Her words came out of the blue. I stopped what I was doing and turned to her, 'What do you mean, there's something wrong?'

She held the letter up; it was almost falling apart, 'This is from Aaron, my eldest. You remember I showed you his photo. Very handsome boy. You know he's evacuated. Near Hertford, he is.'

I'd learned that Ruth sometimes took a while to get to the point.

'That's a long way.' I said, and waited.

'I know I'm a worrier, everyone says so, so perhaps I'm worrying for nothing, but Aaron wrote and he used the code word.'

Now I was really confused. 'The code word?'

She looked around to stop herself crying. 'Before he left I told him if he was unhappy to use a password when he wrote to me. If whoever he lived with was reading his letters, then they wouldn't know what he was up to and treat him even worse. Him and the others.'

'That's really clever, Ruth. What was the password?'

She covered her eyes, 'I'm so silly. I told him to write "there are lots of birds here". That sounds innocent enough.' She waved the letter again, 'And he's written it. But what if there are just a lot of birds and he's forgotten all about the password?'

She was so upset her breathing was haywire.

'Take some deep breaths,' I said, going over to her. 'We'll work out what to do.'

'Would you help?' she said, looking at me as if I were her saviour.

'Of course, but what about your husband?'

She clenched her fists, 'He's so hard to get hold of. You know what it's like in the forces; letters take ages and I don't really know where he is.'

'I thought you said he was in Scotland.'

'He was, but he said something in his last letter that made me think he's been moved. It's so difficult! My little ones! My poor babies!'

On my next day off I went with her to Hertford by coach. It was a Saturday so the Depot office was closed and I'd managed to change my ARP shift to be free. Ruth and I were a little behind schedule and hurried along in the warm sunshine to the coach stop. I tugged off my jacket as we walked, getting in a tangle with my handbag and gas mask.

'Oh dear, what if I need to go to the ladies?' Ruth fretted, 'my bladder, it's not so strong, I might have an accident.'

'Don't have anything to drink until we're almost there. You'll be fine. And they have a toilet break half way there,' I said, hoping it was true.

I spotted our coach at the stop; there were already a lot of people waiting to get on. I looked at my watch. We had a few minutes to make it.

We were the last on so missed the front seats where we would have got the best views of the scenery. We each had a packet of sandwiches and flask of tea ready for the long journey. Ruth had bought extra sandwiches for her children in the hope they would be with us on the return journey. She'd got extra coach tickets too.

For the first half hour Ruth never stopped talking, worrying about anything that could go wrong.

'I didn't tell them I was coming in case they covered up their behaviour. What if they're all out?'

'What if they tell me I'm wrong, and my little ones don't say anything even if they're unhappy?'

'What if we get lost and can't find the house?'

'What if they won't let the children go?'

'What if the children don't love me any more?'

I needed to distract her before her non-stop negativity

drove me crazy. 'How are you getting on with the WVS?' I asked.

My question yanked her out of her worry trance. She looked and me and blinked several times. 'I... ah.. I like it! I have met some lovely people, and it is wonderful to be able to help people.'

I smiled, 'I've been grateful for a WVS cup of tea more than once. I haven't asked you. Are you always in the same place or do you get moved around?'

'Well, I haven't been doing it long so it's always in the rest centre nearest my home, but from next week I'll be going wherever I'm needed.'

'But if your children come with us now, who will look after them when you do your WVS work?'

She patted my arm, 'I've thought of that. I will cut down my shifts to one evening a week and one half day at weekend. My neighbour will look after the children and I will look after her children in return. It's all sorted out. He's a widower and needs help. Sometimes we pool our rations so I can make a nice meal for us all.'

Her voice softened as she spoke about him and I noticed a little smile too, 'What's his name?'

'It's Frank. Short for Franklin, you know.'

I wondered what her husband in Scotland would think about this growing friendship, but it wasn't my place to ask.

Instead, I suggested we eat our sandwiches.

But as we took them out of our bags there was a massive BANG and the coach swerved all over the road, narrowly missing a lorry and a car. The tyres screeched and bags and assorted belongings were thrown all over the place.

'BUGGER! PUNCTURE!' The driver shouted struggling with the steering wheel. We were thrown around left to right and back again several times. We clung on to whatever we could find and my heart raced with fear.

It seemed like ages 'til we screeched to a halt, but it was probably only seconds. The coach finally rested at a strange angle because we'd stopped on the side of the road where the camber was quite steep. And we had a flat tyre too. I hung on to the seat in front to keep me upright although the coach was no-where near on its side. I did a mental check of my body, but nothing was hurt. Ruth clutched my arm, 'Are you okay, my dear?' she said, her voice trembling, 'oh dear, this is terrible. I wish I hadn't got you into this now.'

Before I could answer, the driver stood up. He slid all over the place because of the angle we were at.

'Anyone hurt?' he shouted.

'Yeah, I bumped my head!' someone replied.

'Cut my arm!' someone else called.

'Dropped my sandwiches!' some wit said.

'Lost my dignity!' A voice from the back said.

'Anyone here a doctor?' the driver shouted.

Silence.

'I've had first aid training.' I said, struggling to stand up.

'Thank the Lord for that,' he said, 'will you see to the two what's hurt and I'll change the wheel. It's a slow job.' He turned back to the passengers, 'I'm going to change the tyre, it'll take a while. The weather's not bad so please wait outside while I do it.'

I stopped him, 'Have you got a first aid kit?'

He indicated under his seat, 'It's not much, but it might help.' With that he was gone.

'Better to go outside than sitting all crooked like this.' A woman behind me muttered, getting to her feet, 'you coming, Love?' she asked her husband who'd banged his head.

'No, I'll wait here.' he said, 'I feel a bit wobbly.'

The driver headed to the door.

'If anyone wants to go out, please go now,' I shouted, 'I need to get to the injured.'

About three quarters of the passengers left their seats and I didn't blame them. Although the angle wasn't sharp, it made sitting a strain.

The two who were injured were sitting near each other. 'Right, who's first?' I asked.

The man who'd bumped his head looked at the lady who'd cut her arm, 'See to this lady first, I'm not bleeding.'

The cut on her arm wasn't big, nor was it bleeding profusely. After the awful injuries I'd dealt with on Air Raid duty, I had confidence dealing with it. I'd got the first aid kit and took out a bandage, 'Got a clean hanky?' I asked.

She struggled to get one out of her pocket with the other hand, 'It's more or less clean.' she said apologetically. I used it to press on the cut and then bandaged over it. 'You should probably see a doctor when you get where you're going.'

She pulled a face, 'I 'ave to be a lot worse than that before I can find the dosh to see a doc, but thanks anyway, Love. You done good.'

I smiled and turned to the man. To my horror he had slid between the seats and was unconscious.

'RUTH!' I shouted, 'COME HERE!'

She staggered towards me, the tilt of the bus making her look like a drunk. She took one look at the situation and put her hand to her heart, 'Oy Vey, we need to sort this out quick. Look, he's been a bit sick. I know that's a bad sign.'

I indicated to the cut woman to move away so we had room to move him. It was a struggle. He was a fair size and half under the seat. 'ANY STRONG MEN?' I called out.

'Here!' I heard from outside the coach and felt it move as a big, burly man got back on. He took one look at the situation and turned to me, 'Has he got anything broken?'

I shook my head, 'He said he'd hurt his head, then passed out while I was seeing to someone's cut arm.'

'Okay, leave it to me,' he nudged me aside and bent forward. I couldn't really see exactly how he did it because his bulk filled the space between the seats. But with a few grunts and quiet curses, he got the unconscious man on the seat. 'He's still breathing, but he's out for the count.'

I turned to Ruth, 'Can you go outside and see if there's anyone with him.' I looked around, 'it's seat twenty three.'

She was back very quickly with a worried looking woman, 'What's up?' she said, 'is it my Fred? What's 'appened? Is it that knock on 'is 'ead? Didn't look much.'

'Hang on a minute,' I said, holding her arm, 'Ruth, please ask the driver how long before we get going again.'

She was breathless when she came back, 'He said it's not going well, so it might be an hour.'

I'd seen plenty of head injuries during the Blitz; they couldn't be ignored. 'Right,' I said to the lady who I guessed was his wife, 'this is what we're going to do. Us and this strong man here are going to get Fred outside. We're going to stop a car or lorry and get them to take Fred and you to the nearest hospital. Okay?'

She wrung her hands, 'Really, does it need that? We don't 'ave a lot of money to pay for 'ospitals an' stuff.'

'I'm an ARP Warden so I've got a lot of experience in this sort of thing. If someone is unconscious for a while, they need a doctor as soon as possible.'

She pushed past me and cradled her husband's head in her arms, 'Okay, if you say so, I suppose.' she looked at the big man, 'Will you 'elp please? I can't carry 'im. Wait a mo while I get me bag and coat.'

The big man made his unsteady way to the door carrying Fred over his shoulder like a bag of coal.

Fred's wife and I followed. Ruth had gone on ahead.

When we got outside we found two cars had stopped and the men driving were both telling our driver how to change the wheel. I could see he was gritting his teeth because he knew exactly what to do and didn't need their advice.

'Can one of you men take a patient and his wife to the nearest hospital? He needs to go now. He's got a head injury.'

The shorter one had the bigger car and I was relieved when he spoke up, 'I'll take him, I'm not in a rush.'

Between us we managed to get the injured man on the back seat. He was breathing, but was still unconscious. His wife was twisting her bag in her hands, 'Do you think he'll be okay? I can't manage without him.'

She was about to get in the front seat when Ruth approached her holding her hat. 'We had a little whip-round to help you pay for the hospital,' she said, 'it's not much, but it'll help.'

The lady burst into tears, 'Thank you all so much, I'll never forget this!' Still sobbing, she got in the car and was driven off.

Half an hour later we were on our way again with no inkling of the problems we were about to encounter.

The coach dropped us at Hertford Railway Station. It was a red brick building, long, with two arches at the front and a cupola on the roof.

Ruth got the address of her children out of her handbag and showed me it. 'It's about five miles away. I've got enough money for a taxi.'

But there was no taxi to be found. We went to a railway inspector and asked if buses went there. He looked at the big clock on the station, 'One due in fifteen minutes. Takes a while though. Not far, but it goes all round Will's mother's on the way.'

'I'm getting really nervous now,' Ruth said when he'd gone, 'what if...'

'What if it all goes well?' I interrupted.

She gave a little laugh, 'Silly me, I know, always thinking the worst. Sorry.'

The inspector was right. The five mile journey took near half an hour but we enjoyed looking at the countryside and attractive villages. They made a welcome change from war-torn London.

The village green was so pretty it could have been on a chocolate box. Triangular, it had thatched cottages along one side and a mixture of old buildings on another. The road completed the triangle. Ducks wandered around the green, while others swam lazily on the pond in the middle.

Ruth looked again at the address, 'Bengeo Road,' she said, 'we'll have to ask, all the road signs are gone.'

A bent elderly man wearing a flat cap was walking his equally ancient dog who, despite his age, still had to be pulled back from chasing the ducks.

Ruth approached him, 'Do you know where Bengeo Road is, please?' she asked with a sweet smile.

The man chuckled, 'It's right behind you, me dear. That road there.' He pointed directly behind us. 'Mind, it's a long road.' He stopped talking as an army lorry went past, belching exhaust fumes. For a moment the scene smelled more like Deptford than a country village. 'We don't get many strangers hereabouts. You come to visit your children? They evacuated here? My daughter and her friend have taken in two girls from London. They're having a wonderful time. Their mums get here whenever they can. Cry their eyes out, but they know their little ones are well looked after. That's the main thing. Nasty place London at the moment,' he pulled at his dog's lead again, 'what number Bengeo Road did you want?'

'It's not a number, it's Midway Farm. My children are evacuated there.'

He went very quiet, and a frown crossed his already wrinkled brow. 'It's about a mile up there on the left. I shouldn't say this, my dear, but you want to be careful with them. John and Betty Godfrey they are. Keep themselves to themselves, but they aren't too popular round here.'

Ruth's shoulders sagged, 'Why's that?'

'I don't rightly know, but they seem to upset a lot of people. Never had nothing to do with them myself so I can't speak from experience. They say he's not too bad, but her...' he left the sentence hanging.

I put my arm through Ruth's, 'Thank you for the warning. I think we'd better be heading off there.'

We dragged our feet for the first minute or two, then I straightened up, 'Come on, Ruth, we're doing nothing wrong. Let's make sure you've understood the code properly and bring your little ones home if they're unhappy.'

We walked a little faster, past some tumbledown barns; cows; crops we couldn't identify and lovely blue and yellow wild flowers. A bird flew close overhead, its beak full of tiny twigs.

'Do you think we should sneak in and just grab them?' Ruth asked.

'Why should we do that? They're your kids, you can collect them any time you like.'

'But I haven't given any warning or anything. They might be angry.'

I stopped and looked her straight in the face, 'Ruth, we'll be okay. There might be a few unpleasant moments, but it'll soon be over. Think about having them home with you.'

The road began to be lined with trees and we came across the sign to the farm unexpectedly. My feet were already beginning to ache and I mentally groaned when I saw the long lane to the farmhouse and barns.

Two men were mending a fence and nodded as we went past. Then we spotted a third who was bending down nailing some wire.

'Aaron!' Ruth screamed and ran forward, arms outstretched.

His jaw dropped open, 'Mum? Is that you?' he bent down and wriggled between the wires, smiling widely.

The man he was with took off his cap and scratched his head, 'You his mum, then? Does the missus know you're coming? She don't like surprises, you know. Not a bit.'

Ruth nodded to him, her arms wrapped around Aaron, 'Did you mean that, about the birds?' she asked him.

He nodded and whispered something in her ear. She turned to me, a look of determination setting her mouth in a straight line. 'Come on, we're going to get the other two.'

We marched up the lane, looking left and right for the farm owners. Farm smells followed us: cow manure; compost; and hay fighting to outdo each other.

'The boss'll be in the milking shed this time of day,' Aaron said, his arm through hers, 'her... she'll be feeding the hens or getting the dinner ready.'

'What about your sisters?' Ruth asked, almost out of breath from walking so fast.

'She gives them all sorts of jobs. Scrubbing the floors; cleaning out the chicken run; peeling spuds; washing the clothes. And they get a clout round the ears if they don't do it right. I do, too.' He grabbed her arm tighter, 'Mum, you've got to get us away from here! It's horrible. Judith cries herself to sleep every night.'

Ruth leaned over and kissed his cheek, 'Why didn't you tell me before?'

'She reads all our letters, and anyway I was scared she'd see through our code. She's really scary, Mum.'

We approached the farm yard and house. Skinny chickens pecked the ground and old broken down farm equipment covered in weeds lay along one side of the path. A little way off we heard cows mooing, and a pig grunting. The patch in front of the house was muddy and neglected. As we got nearer we heard, 'DO THAT AGAIN, BETTER THIS TIME OR YOU'LL FEEL THE SIDE OF MY HAND!'

The three of us ran in to find little Judith scrubbing the stone floor. She was on her hands and knees and her back sagged. Her hair hung loose and needed washing. Behind her an ancient Welsh dresser held an assortment of crockery.

'Who the hell are you?' the woman spat the words out as we walked through the door. Her beefy hands rested on her generous hips.

Judith continued to scrub, although I saw her back tense.

'I'm Judith's mum...' before she could finish her sentence Judith dropped the scrubbing brush and turned around.

'Mum? Mum?' she ran and threw her arms round Ruth's legs. 'are we going home now?'

'No, you're not.' Mrs Godfrey said, slapping her hand on

the scarred kitchen table, 'that hasn't been arranged, and you ain't finished that floor yet. Not by a long way.'

Ruth clung on to Judith, 'Where's my Miriam?'

Mrs Godfrey picked up a broom and held it in front of her like a weapon. She looked ready to hit Ruth with it.

Ruth's jaw jutted forward, 'I said, where's Miriam?'

'They call her Mary,' Aaron said, 'they think Miriam is too Jewish. They call me Adam.'

Ruth took a step forward, 'How dare you! You.. You... Now. Where is Miriam?'

'You can't just take them you know,' the woman said with a smug smile, 'it has to be sorted with the welfare people.'

Ruth's eyes narrowed and she glared at her, 'Sod the welfare people. Did you arrange to treat my children badly? Do they know about that? Now, tell me where Miriam is.'

Mrs. Godfrey clutched the broom so tight that her knuckles went white. Her lips formed a tight line. 'Find her yourself.'

Aaron moved towards the door, 'I'll get her, I know where she'll be.'

Ruth turned to Judith, 'Go and get your things. We're going home.'

'She can't take them!' the woman hissed, 'I got some of them.'

Judith stood frozen, not knowing who to obey.

'Go get them, Judith,' Ruth said, 'I'll sort this out.'

She waited until Judith left the room then turned to the angry woman, 'You've been paid for having my kids, and looking at the state of this place,' she waved her arm to indicate the state of the kitchen, 'you won't have spent much on anything. I'll be reporting you. You'll never have another child lodged with you. Ever.'

Red with fury, Mrs Godfrey swung the broom towards

Ruth, but she reckoned without my army training. I stepped between them and grabbed the broom before it did any harm. For that moment I felt invincible. I yanked it out of her hands, banged it on the doorframe so hard it broke in two and then I threw the bits in the muddy yard. 'You won't be needing that,' I said, 'and don't think of trying anything else or you'll see what the army has trained me to do.'

Before she could answer Aaron came back with Miriam. Like the others she threw herself at her mother, tears rolling down her face,

'Mum... mum... it's really you...' she kept repeating.

Ruth hugged her so tight she could hardly breathe. 'Now, the pair of you, go and get your stuff. Judith is already up there. Be double quick about it. We want to get out of here within five minutes.'

They ran out of the room and Ruth and I both faced Mrs Godfrey, 'You can't...' she started, her fists clenched.

'DON'T YOU TELL ME WHAT I CAN'T DO!' Ruth hissed. 'You should be ashamed of yourself, you... you... utter bitch!'

I gaped, I'd never heard Ruth using a single cuss word before, never mind calling people names. I was delighted she did. Mrs Godfrey deserved it and more.

Ruth backed towards the stairs, never taking her eyes off the woman. She opened the door and called up, 'Hurry, kids, we need to leave now.'

Two minutes later there was a clattering down the stairs and all three came in holding their cardboard cases. Judith was clutching her threadbare Teddy Bear, its bright pink ribbon worn thin with rubbing. All three wore gas masks over their shoulders.

'Come on, little ones,' Ruth said holding out her hands.

The two girls clung on to her and Aaron, to my surprise, reached out for mine. I held it tight.

We backed out of the door as if expecting to be attacked any minute.

'I haven't got my coat!' Judith cried, 'she'll tell me off.'

'She'll never tell you off for anything ever again,' Ruth said, 'you'll never see her again, and we'll find you another coat.'

We ran out of the yard followed by a barrage of curses from Mrs Godfrey. But I was glad she didn't run after us. Aaron was pulling me ahead, and I had to tell him to slow down to the speed Judith could manage.

'We must get away, we need to get away!' he repeated again and again.

We almost made it to the road when we heard the rattle of an old tractor turning into the yard.

'That's him, the boss,' Aaron said.

The tractor more or less blocked our path.

'What's going on here, then?' the farmer said, getting down from his tractor, 'making a run for it, are you?'

I stepped forward, still holding Aaron. 'Yes, we are. We're taking these children home and you're not going to stop us.'

To my surprise he stepped back, 'No skin off my nose. Useless little buggers. Next time we'll get kids what can earn their keep proper like.'

Now Ruth stepped forward, 'There'll never be a next time. I'll make sure of that!'

He simply shrugged as we stepped past him, wriggled round the tractor and out on the road.

We ran for the first few hundred yards, almost pulling little Judith along. But then we realised we weren't being followed and whooped with triumph. We skipped and hopped a little way, then our energy seemed to drain and we walked the rest of the way into the village.

The old man was sitting on a bench on the village green and he stood up as he saw us appear. He was smiling broadly, 'The escape committee! Well done!' He shook hands with Miriam and Aaron and gently pinched Judith's cheek. 'I'm very glad to see you young people and I bet you're pleased to see your mum,' he looked at us, 'any trouble?'

Ruth and I looked at each other. 'Could have been worse.' I said.

CHAPTER 12

I walked into our living room, barely able to drag my feet. The physical and emotional effects of getting Ruth's children from the awful farmer's wife left me exhausted. So the last thing I wanted was Bronwyn's first words,

'You've got a telegram!'

I sank into the chair, my heart sinking. Telegrams usually meant bad news; death, injury or capture. I didn't dare look at the envelope she was waving.

'It's all right, he's not dead, Cariad!' she said with a smile, 'I looked! I could see through the envelope it didn't have a black edge.'

The tension drained out of me like water from a tap. I held out my hand, too tired to even tell her off for opening my post.

Without a word I unfolded it:

WILL MEET YOU AT YOUR DEPOT AT FIVE THIRTY
TOMORROW. EDWARD.

My heart beat fast. Edward, my fiancé, coming next day!

Bronwyn grinned, 'Want me to do your hair in the morning?'

'No point, my cap will ruin it anyway, but thanks for the offer. I'll wash it before I go to bed. Where's Marion?'

'She's gone to the pictures with her mum. That way her dad doesn't have to know about it.'

She'd hardly finished her sentence when we heard a key in the door and Marion came in.

She shrugged off her coat, which barely buttoned up over her stomach. 'How did you get on with Ruth? Did you get the children?' she asked.

'It all went well; they're all safe and sound. I'll tell you the details tomorrow. Mind you, Edward's coming tomorrow so who know what will happen!'

Marion smiled, 'Bronwyn told me. I'm so pleased for you, you must be so excited. I hope we get to meet him.'

I yawned and stretched my arms, 'I think I'm too tired to be excited. Before I go to bed, tell me how it went with your mum.'

Marion reached into her bag and pulled out a delicate white baby cardigan. She wiped away a tear, 'Look what she made. It's so beautiful,' she rubbed it against her cheek, 'She's so upset that I can't keep the baby. She keeps trying to find ways round it, but none of them work.'

I took the cardigan from her and inspected the exquisite pattern and tiny buttons. 'It's beautiful, Marion. I hope your baby's new parents keep it and pass it on. It's obvious it was made with love.'

Marion took it from me and carefully wrapped it in tissue paper. 'I'm going to write a letter as well. I don't know if the new parents will give it to my baby, but I'd like to think they will.'

I gave her a hug, 'That's a wonderful idea. You're very thoughtful, Marion,' I yawned again, 'Right, excuse me girls, I'm off to the lavvy, then it's bed for me, it's been a long day.'

I tore off a piece of newspaper to use as toilet paper, when a picture on it caught my eye. It was an old newspaper, one of the dusty pile we inherited when we moved in. The photo showed several Blackshirts marching. Just looking at the Fascists gave me the shivers. They were far-right anti-semitics. Most people were relieved when their Union was disbanded. There was something familiar about the man on the right that made me look closer.

I squinted and looked closely. My first impression was right. It was Mr Biggerstaff, the man who provided goods for the Depot.

My tiredness vanished and I soon hurried back into the living room. 'Look at this!' I said to Bronwyn who was tidying up for the night, 'It's Biggerstaff, he's a Blackshirt!'

Marion frowned, 'But I thought they didn't exist any more.'

Bronwyn took the newspaper cutting from me, 'They don't, but you can bet some of them still have the horrible ideas they used to have,' she looked at me.

I took the cutting from her. Mr McDonald needed to see it.

'If he is still a fascist you've got to wonder if he's up to no good at the Depot,' Marion said.

We all sat down again, 'What could he do?' I wondered.

We were all silent for a minute, 'He could provide dodgy goods,' Bronwyn said, 'what does he supply anyway?'

I thought back to the dockets I'd seen, 'I don't really know, they're just code numbers.'

'If they're guns he could do something so they don't work properly,' Marion said.

'Or if it's food, he could poison some of it.'

'Or he could be in league with someone else. If he's a Nazi sympathiser, he'll be doing something to help them win the war.'

We talked round and round it for several minutes, but got no further.

'Can I ask you two to try to notice anything suspicious,' I said.

Despite being so tired, I lay in bed wide awake. I wondered what it could mean if Mr Biggerstaff was a fascist. Could he be plotting against the Depot and the army in some way? Or perhaps those days were behind him and his beliefs had changed. The questions rolled round and round in my mind, but there were no answers without more information. I turned to reliving the events at Midfield Farm and the coach breakdown. I was almost asleep when I realised I'd thought about all these things, but not about seeing Edward next day. I couldn't understand why I wasn't as excited as I'd always been in the past; not that we saw each other very often.

But it was hard to concentrate on anything next day - I constantly looked at the clock and counted off the hours until Edward arrived. My typing was so bad, I wasted more paper than Ruth. She wasn't there to compete with though, because she was spending the day sorting out her children. I guessed it would take a while for them to settle back at home and feel safe again.

Finally five thirty arrived. The cover was already on my typewriter, my hair was combed, my lipstick freshly applied. I saw Edward arrive at the gate and speak to the guard. He looked as handsome as ever. He was still using his walking stick, but leaning on it less heavily. The guard soon waved him in.

'He's here!' I shouted and ran out of the room.

'Don't do anything I wouldn't do!' Bronwyn shouted after me.

Edward's greeting wasn't what I expected. He gave a thin smile and a feeble hug, but didn't take my hand. Frowning, I said, 'Want to come and meet the others?' I grabbed his hand and tried to pull him towards the office.

'Not now, Lily. I need to talk to you privately.'

Puzzled, I ran in and picked up my stuff. Bronwyn and Marion looked up, expecting to see Edward with me.

'What's up, Cariad?' Bronwyn said, 'you look like you've lost a pound and found a penny.'

'Tell you later,' I said. I grabbed my coat, gas mask and bag and ran back out again.

Edward looked as serious as ever. 'Let's go somewhere where we can talk. I saw a pub round the corner that wasn't crowded.'

I wanted to ask what it was about but I was too scared. He must want to break off our engagement, I thought. There was no other explanation. He'd met someone else and fallen in love, or his feelings for me had changed while we were apart. Our letters to each other had tailed off lately and I hadn't heard from him for a couple of weeks, but that wasn't unusual with army mail. I walked beside him, not touching, my hands clammy and elbows close to my body.

We stopped at The Eagle, a pub in a side street, and went to the quietest corner. A noisy group of men were in the other bar, but we could still hear each other speak.

'Shandy?' Edward asked, and walked to the bar without waiting for an answer.

I sat down and took my coat off. I trembled as I watched him give the order and it seemed for ever until he came back.

I could keep silent no longer, and the second he sat down I asked him what was wrong.

He looked into his pint, took a long quaff then half turned to me, 'When were you going to tell me?'

I frowned, 'Tell you what?'

'You know. When were you going to tell me?'

'I have no idea what you're talking about. Edward, be clear! What is it?'

He avoided my eye again, 'Our baby. When were you going to tell me you're giving it away? Or is it someone else's?'

'What baby? Someone else's? What on earth are you talking about?' I reached for his hand, but he jerked his away.

Then, before he answered, the penny dropped. His friend who had seen me with Marion at the mother-and-baby home in Colchester. And jumped to the wrong conclusion.

'Are you talking about your friend who saw me in Colchester? Did he tell you where I was?'

'Yes he did, and I can't believe you didn't tell me about it.'

I gave him a death stare, 'What? Break a confidence and tell you I'd gone with a friend who needs to get her baby adopted? Hmmm? Is that it? And what do you bloody mean by "someone else's"? I had no idea you had such a low opinion of me.'

Outraged, I stood up, picked up my shandy, threw it in his face, snatched up my things and walked out without looking back. I was so angry I could hardly breathe. How dare he think of me like that? Then a nasty little voice reminded me that when I thought he was dead I'd spent a night with a wonderful colleague from the Air Raid team. But that was then! I argued with myself. I wasn't being unfaithful because I thought he was dead. I was amazed that Edward would jump to conclusions without asking me first.

I twisted my engagement ring and wriggled it off my finger. I looked down at it for a minute. Should I throw it back in his face? Sell it and keep the money? Throw it away? I pushed my arm back to hurl it as far as I could, but before I could fling it my hand was grabbed.

'Lily, I'm sorry,' Edward said, forcing my hand closed, 'I'm an idiot. Forgive me. My friend was so convinced it was you at the home in Colchester - maybe he didn't see your friend. When he told me I was consumed with anger and jealousy.'

But I wasn't listening, I was too furious. I thrust the ring into his hand and ran off, knowing he wouldn't be able to catch up with me.

When I got home I threw my bag and gas masks down and collapsed into a chair, tears streaming down my face.

Marion came over and took my hand, 'What is it? Is it something to do with Edward?'

'You were right! That bloke we saw in Colchester thought it was me having the baby and told Edward. He was upset because he thought I hadn't told him and was getting his baby adopted. I can't believe he'd think that of me.'

Then I realised what I'd said. I paused and blew my nose, 'Marion, I'm so sorry, I didn't mean anything bad about you.'

The corners of her mouth turned down, 'I'd deserve it if you did.'

'No, you wouldn't, you don't deserve what's happened to you. You just ended up with the wrong man and it looks like I did too. I can't believe he'd think I wouldn't tell him if something like that was happening to me. He doesn't know me at all.'

'Some blokes...'

'I know. Some blokes are rotters, but I thought he was one of the good ones. Well, I've given him his ring back...'

'You haven't!'

'I have. We're finished!'

CHAPTER 13

A couple of days later I had a letter from Edward. My first thought was to tear it up without reading it, but something stopped me. Instead I prowled round it as if it would bite me. Had I been too hasty breaking off our engagement? I tried to count the number of days we'd spent together in all the months since we met. I couldn't remember them all, but I judged it wasn't more than thirty five and many of those were only part days. If we'd had those thirty days one after the other when we met, people would think we were crazy getting engaged so quickly. That old saying about Marry in Haste, Repent at Leisure, came into my mind. Perhaps we been too hasty getting engaged.

Eventually I picked up the letter and sat down, turning it over and over in my hands.

'Don't be so stupid!' I said out loud, and finally tore it open.

Dearest Lily,

I am writing to ask you to forgive me for my behaviour when we met this week. I should have had more trust in you, because I know you are a trustworthy person. It was a terrible thing for me to do. I was so upset by what my friend said, I just wasn't thinking straight.

I have to go back to my base later today or I would wait here for a reply in the hope of seeing you, but hope you will write soon.

Your

Edward

I tore the letter into small pieces and thew the bits in the bin. Strangely, I felt a pang of relief that I couldn't explain.

CHAPTER 14

Two nights later I arrived home and was about to open our front door when one of the arty neighbours called out to me, 'Hey, we're having a little get together tonight. Why don't you come? Very informal.'

She was older than me, probably about forty, and her hair was tied in a crazy bun on top of her head. An emerald green pencil stuck out of it. She wore a bright purple loose dress that I think was called a Kaftan. There were yellow and white magic symbols all around the hem and tiny bells attached to a neck tie.

A night out was just what I needed to stop me thinking about breaking up with Edward.

'Can I bring my friends?' I called back.

She grinned, 'Of course, the more the merrier. See you later. About an hour? I'm Vanessa by the way.'

As I stepped into the hallway, I bumped into Wendy from upstairs who was heading out. 'Just getting some fresh air,' she said, 'How are you?'

'I'm well. Is your husband away at the moment?' I hadn't

heard any rows or his heavy footsteps on the stairs for several days.

She hitched her bag higher on her shoulder, 'Yes, not sure how long for this time. It's a bit lonely when he's not here.'

'Maybe I can help with that,' I said, 'Vanessa, the lady next door, just invited us in. They're having a little do tonight. She said I could take friends. Would you like to come? They said it's informal so no need to dress up.'

She looked surprised at the invitation, 'Really? I could come? That'd be great. I'd love to get to know all of you more. I meant to ask, have you got a friend staying at the moment? I've seen someone else coming in and out.'

I could hardly deny it, 'Marion. She's staying for a little while until she sorts out somewhere else to stay. She got bombed out, poor thing.'

An hour later, Wendy, Marion and I knocked on Vanessa's door. Bronwyn was on ambulance duty; she'd be upset at missing this opportunity but there was no way round it. There'd been no air raid sirens for a couple of nights, and we hoped the Nazi bombers were away in Russia like the newspapers said.

Vanessa was still wearing the purple kaftan, but now she had her hair in a matching turban. Silver bracelets jangled on each arm. I felt very dowdy in the green second-hand dress I'd got from the Rest Centre. Wendy looked quite formal in a fitted red dress with a gold necklace. Marion wore the loosest dress she had, 'One of them kaftans would be good for me,' she whispered.

Although the house was built the same as the one we were in, it couldn't have looked more different. Bright rugs covered every floor in the living room and hall, and the ceiling was draped in a golden silky fabric. It looked like pictures I'd seen in a book about the Arabian Nights. And there was a strange smell too; sort of sweet and woody. 'What's that smell?' I whispered to Wendy.

'It's incense. Thomas and I were posted to India for a while - you get used to the smell there.'

Vanessa introduced us to her friends. Timothy was a lot older than her and wore black trousers, a claret coloured smoking jacket and pink cravat. He had a cigarette holder and was smoking a black cigarette. Amanda, Vanessa's daughter, wore a kaftan as well, but hers was black with silver and gold magical patterns.

Catherine was about eighty and her arms and hands were brown and stringy like an old piece of dehydrated leather. Her smile was warm and welcoming. She stood up slowly, and gave each of us a hug. 'I hope you'll find the evening enlightening, my dears,' she said. She was dressed entirely in black and had a silver ring on each finger and thumb.

'Do sit down,' Vanessa said when she'd done the introductions, 'what can I get you to drink? We have home made wine, some elderflower cordial or tea.'

Jazz was playing softly in the background as we held our drinks. The conversation soon turned to the bombing and the hardships of rationing. Looking around at these well fed and comfortably off people, it was difficult to imagine them having any hardships.

Vanessa sat on a rocking chair, leaning back on a bright turquoise velvet cushion, 'We meet every few weeks and like to have a theme for our evenings,' she explained, 'we've all known each other for years, and a theme stops us talking about the war or our aches and pains all the time.'

'Hear, hear!' Timothy said, 'we've already said more than enough. Mind you, my knees still...'

'What's tonight's theme?' Amanda quickly asked, although she must have known already.

'The supernatural. Catherine has a real gift for fortune telling, and we can all take part in a seance.' She looked at her watch, 'a medium, Madam Loretta, will be here shortly to conduct it. She has a reputation for being genuine. You don't have to take part if you don't want to. Oh, and we'll have ghost stories! It's just a bit of a laugh really,' she looked at the three of us, 'Is that okay with you? If you'd rather come round another night, we'd quite understand.'

It sounded like good fun to me. I'd seen a fortune teller's tent at a fairground, but never had the nerve to go in. And I'd seen a seance in a

film once. I looked at Marion and Wendy. They were a bit hesitant, but nodded agreement.

Vanessa clapped her hands, 'That's all good then. Now, where shall we start? I suggest we do this in sort of shifts. We can tell or read ghost stories, but anyone who would rather have their fortune told can go into the other room with Catherine. How does that sound?'

'What about the seance?' Timothy asked.

'We can do that last. We'll all be well fortified with alcohol by then,' she clapped her hands, 'Now, let's prepare the atmosphere for the evening.'

It took ages to set the room up because no-one was in a hurry. There were still plenty of aches and pains, and gossip about friends, to talk about. The blackout curtains were already in place. Vanessa pulled out a side table, fiddled with a leg and it opened into a round table. Timothy pulled the velvet cover off his chair and draped it over the table ready for the seance. Amanda took a dozen candles out of a cupboard. That impressed me; they were hard to come by.

We soon had full glasses in our hands, and a plate of vegetable nibbles in front of us.

'Right,' Vanessa said, 'let's get organised. Who wants their fortune told?'

There was a moment's silence then Timothy spoke, 'Oh, go on, I'll do it, there's a first time for everything.'

'Right, anyone else?'

Marion raised her hand a couple of inches, 'Is that a yes?' Vanessa asked.

Marion nodded, her cheeks pink, 'Does it have to be private? Can Lily come in with me?'

Catherine smiled, 'Of course,' she turned to me, 'I would ask you to sit to one side and remain completely silent no matter what you see or hear. Is that all right?'

'Why don't you go first?' Timothy asked, 'I'm in no hurry.'

Marion, Catherine and I went into the dining room. The wallpaper and curtains matched, with a muted amber flower design. They looked very old, even Victorian, and worn through in places. Lighter patches on the walls showed where paintings had been. It was plainer than the front room; a lot plainer. A dining table and six ageing chairs were in the middle of the room, and a battered side table and a plant stand with an aspidistra stood in the corners. Catherine noticed me looking around, 'They move house quite often so they don't like too many belongings. Too much stuff tends to clutter the mind.'

There was a black cloth on the table, and on top of that something covered with a bright purple and pink silk scarf.

'Come and sit opposite me,' she said to Marion, 'and Lily, why don't you move one of the chairs over to the corner where you won't be in either of our eye lines. We don't want to get distracted, do we?'

She lit a thick white candle and an incense stick on the side table behind her chair and turned off the electric light. The smell of the incense and the dim lighting gave the room an immediate atmosphere, both calming and yet somehow unsettling.

'I use a crystal ball for fortune telling,' she said, indicating the bump under the scarf, 'but first I like to hold something belonging to the sitter. Do you have something I can use, Marion?'

Marion hesitated, and looked round as if she was thinking better of the whole thing. Then she gave a small shrug, took off a ring, and passed it to Catherine. Catherine held it for a minute or two with her eyes closed, then she returned it.

'Thank you, dear, now let's get on.'

She removed the scarf, uncovering the crystal ball. It rested on a low wooden stand with carved elephants on each corner. She said a few words, so low I couldn't hear them, then held the ball in her hands. For two or three minutes she looked steadily into it without saying a word. The only sound was the low hum of the story telling from the next room. Then she placed the ball on the little wooden holder and pulled it closer to herself. She waved her hands in front of it two or three times. She hadn't begun speaking yet, and already my mouth was dry and I heard my pulse pounding in my ears. I wondered if Marion was feeling the same.

'The mist is clearing,' Catherine said, and her voice, although quiet, made me jump, 'I can tell security is one of your main aims in life,' she looked up at Marion, who nodded.

'There is movement. It's not clear if this is to do with

where you live, work or relationships. But things will not stay the same for you.'

Marion was obviously pregnant so that wasn't a surprising thing to say. And most people wanted security. I was beginning to think this was all a hoax - I'd read about fortune tellers who said things that applied to everyone.

I was soon to change my mind.

Catherine went quiet again, looking unblinkingly at the ball which seemed to pulse and glow in the dim candle light.

'Your baby will be a girl. Small, but a healthy girl. I see movement again.' There was another long pause. 'The mists are swirling again, but you will have a sorrow that will live with you for the rest of your life. And yet,' another pause, 'there will be a surprise solution to a problem, but I can't tell what it is. But you will find other happiness in life, and good things will happen for you in the future. Many consolations.'

She continued to look at the ball, but it gradually dimmed and she looked up. 'I'm afraid the pictures have gone now. I can't control them. Did any of that make sense to you, Dear?' she asked Marion.

Marion's bottom lip trembled, 'I understand the sorrow, but not the rest.'

Catherine reached across the table and took her hand, 'Those things are in the future, so you cannot know what they are yet. But that news is good. You have much to look forward to.'

We all stood up, but I noticed that Marion looked a bit shaky, 'I think I'll go home if you don't mind. That's enough for one evening.'

'Do you want me to come with you?' I asked.

She shook her head, 'No, I'll be fine. I'll have an early night. Thank you for the reading, Catherine.'

Catherine walked round the table and hugged Marion, 'Be

of good cheer. Today's unhappiness will gradually fade away. I'll see you to the door.'

The doorbell rang soon after. 'That'll be Madam Loretta. By the way if you can afford it, we'll pay her a shilling each.'

Wendy stood up, 'Catherine, can I have my fortune told?'

Timothy waved an arm, 'You go ahead, I'm not too worried if we never get to me.'

The two of them went into the back room as Madam Loretta came into the living room. I was expecting someone exotic; perhaps a dark skinned woman with masses of long wavy black hair and a gypsy scarf round her head with little metal discs hanging over her forehead. And a foreign accent. And high heeled shoes. Instead she was a plump, short woman with greying hair - everyone's granny. When she took off her black coat which was a little too tight, she was wearing a black skirt, a green jumper and flat black shoes. No magic symbols in sight.

''ello, Ducks,' she said, in a broad London accent, 'Lovely to see you all. Any chance of a Rosie Lea before we start? I'm right parched. Biscuit too if you've got one,' she looked around, 'nice to see you've got the room ready and everything.'

She plonked herself down on an armchair and rummaged around in her large handbag. Vanessa left to make her tea. 'I met Vanessa before when she came to one of my seances 'er friend 'ad. I 'ad a message for 'er from her grannie.' She took out a notebook and pencil, 'now, who are you all? Just tell me your names. I'll write them down 'cos I've got a shocking memory. Shocking, it is. Don't tell me anything else because otherwise if the spirits come through with a message or two you'll think I'm on the fiddle.'

We all gave our names and chatted about the bombings until Vanessa came back, 'I've told Catherine and Wendy not to come back in until we've finished. I didn't think you'd want to be interrupted.'

Madam Loretta took the cup and saucer from her, and two biscuits from the tea plate. 'That's right, the spirits will take fright if we're interrupted and we'll never get them back. Let's 'ope there's no air raids tonight neither.'

'Now,' she said, looking round, 'are you all going to attend? It can be a bit, well scary, if you've never been before. Mind you, sometimes the spirits never come through at all. Other times two or three are fighting in my head to give messages for different people. Fair gives me a 'eadache, that do.'

'Do they tell you terrible things?' I asked, remembering what Catherine had just told Marion.

Madam Loretta brushed a biscuit crumb from her jumper, 'Not as such, no. But sometimes they give a warning, like. Seems like most of 'em can't see in the future though. More often they just come through to let their loved one know they're 'appy where they are. Or where to find something they've lost. It brings a lot of comfort to the bereaved.'

When she'd finished her tea, she sat at the table and indicated to join her, 'I don't mind where you sit, Ducks. Any of you drunk, by the way? The vibrations won't be right if you are.'

Vanessa spoke up, 'Timothy and I had a couple of glasses of wine earlier ,but we're not drunk.'

Madam Loretta smiled, 'That's okay, then.'

I sat opposite her, Amanda to my right and Vanessa and Timothy sat either side of her. She fished in her bag again and produced a thick candle, 'Let's 'ave this instead of them lights. They're too bright for the spirits and we won't get any messages.'

She lit the candle and Vanessa turned off the light. The

only other light was the tiny glow of the incense stick. We could hear the quiet voices of Catherine and Wendy in the next room and the occasional car going past, but otherwise it was quiet.

'Now, all 'old 'ands, and close your peepers,' Madam Loretta said, 'I like to say a little prayer before we start.'

I felt a bit stupid holding hands, and still wasn't sure I believed a word of all this. Madam Loretta closed her eyes and spoke pleadingly.

'Spirits, please surround me with Divine light. Bring my team of guides, Angels and Ascended Masters, with the Archangels and angels who can offer the most support now. Surround me fully and completely with a protective white light.'

I cheated and opened one eye a bit. To my surprise she did have a very slight white light surrounding her. I decided it must be an optical illusion or a trick, but it spooked me out a bit and I shivered.

She opened her eyes again and smiled, back to her granny self. 'Right, before we start I just remembered something,' she delved into her bag again and produced some crystals which she placed around the candle. 'These'll 'elp protect us an' all, we don't want any bad spirits visiting us, do we? Right, I'm going to call my favourite spirit now, a lady what's been dead 'undreds of years, Mary 'er name is. She 'elps me reach the spirits for my customers. That's you. Anyone 'oping for a message tonight?'

There was silence for a minute, then Timothy spoke, 'I'd like to know if my close friend, Duncan, is happy where he is.'

'Righty oh, Ducks. I'll do my best. Anyone else?'

No-one else spoke.

'I sense the spirits in a lot of different ways. Mostly

voices, but sometimes I see 'em, or even smell 'em so don't be surprised if I wrinkles me nose.'

She looked around and decided we were ready.

'Okay, then. 'Old 'ands again. No need to close your eyes, but keep 'olding 'ands no matter what 'appens. You'll disturb the spirits otherwise.'

We sat quietly for a minute and then she said, 'Repeat after me. Spirits we call upon you to bring messages to those gathered here.'

We repeated that bit, then, 'Spirits we come in goodwill and would love to 'ear your messages.'

We repeated all of that three times.

'Good spirit, Mary,' she called, 'come to me now in safety and love. 'Elp me to give messages to the people around this table.'

We waited without saying a word although we glanced at each other. In the candle-light it was difficult to make out expressions on people's faces.

Madam Loretta suddenly gasped and looked towards the ceiling. 'Is that you, Mary? Welcome, thank you for coming tonight. My friend Timothy is present and would like a message from his friend Duncan if he agrees to grace us with his presence. Can you find Duncan? Is he willing to give a message to Timothy?'

For a minute or two she held her head forward to one side as if she was listening, 'I 'ear a man's voice. Is that you, Duncan?' she paused, 'yes? Duncan is 'ere. What message do you 'ave for Timothy, Duncan?'

It might have been the flickering light; but her face seemed to change. It was like someone was playing games with the muscles in her cheeks, her forehead and her mouth so she was still Madam Loretta, and yet also someone else.

'Timothy, Sweetheart!' she said in a loud and jovial man's voice, completely unlike her own.

Timothy started and almost broke away from the circle. 'Duncan? Is that really you?' he sobbed, 'Are you happy where you are?' he finally asked.

'I'd be a lot better with you here to cuddle me!' 'Duncan said with a dirty chuckle that filled the room, 'I miss you. Every bit of you - you know what I mean.'

It might have been almost dark, but I could feel myself getting pink listening to this.

'I miss you, too,' Timothy whispered, 'there's never been anyone else since you.'

There was another deep throated chuckle, 'Do you remember that time when we were on that beach in Brighton...'

Timothy spluttered, 'We don't need to talk about that now, Duncan!'

'Oh, a pity, that was such a good...'

'Yes, yes.' Timothy interrupted, 'Let's talk about some-thing else. Will you be waiting for me?

'Of course I'll be waiting for you. We'll be together when you pass over. We can row and kiss and make-up like we always did.'

Timothy sagged, 'That's wonderful to know. Thank you, Duncan, I don't think it will be long before I join you.'

Duncan's voice began to fade, 'See you soon, Sweetie, don't do anything I wouldn't do...'

Madam Loretta's body relaxed, 'Duncan, are you still there?' she paused and listened again then shook her head, 'Duncan's gone, I'm afraid, I 'ope that was some comfort to you Timothy. Now, let's see if there's anyone else.' She looked up again, listening, 'Mary, do you 'ave any other messages for anyone 'ere from the spirits?'

She listened again for a minute or two, 'I'm getting an old lady, I can see 'er this time. She's short and very thin; 'er hair is grey and she's wearing a blue felt 'at. She says 'er name is Minnie. Does that mean anything to anyone?'

I felt a tingle run down my spine, 'It might be my grannie. She passed over a few years ago.'

Madam Loretta spoke again, 'Are you Lily's grannie, Minnie?' she waited for a response only she could hear. Then,

'Lil, my dear,' she said in an old ladies voice that could have been my granny's, 'I have watched you as you've grown up and I'm so proud of you, but I've come to tell you you're in danger.'

A long pause,

'What do you mean, granny?' I asked, a catch in my voice.

'I can't tell exactly, it's not clear to me, but there's a big man and a church. You must take care, your life will be in danger.'

Wendy and I left at the same time, and went into our flat for a cup of tea. Marion was still awake although in her nightie and dressing gown.

'What did Catherine say to you, Wendy?' I asked.

Wendy frowned, 'Well, it was really odd. Most of it was, well, a bit of nothing. But then she said I would get bad news and it would be the best news I've ever had. How does that make sense?'

We talked round it, but couldn't make sense of it either. 'Either of you get any messages?' she asked, drinking the last of her tea.

'My granny came through,' I said, 'and warned me I'd be

in danger. Something to do with a big man and a church. I've no idea what she meant, I expect it's all made up.'

'She told me I'd have great sadness.' Marion said.

Wendy put her cup and saucer down on the floor, 'I hope that's not bad news about your husband. Do you hear from him often?'

Marion could hardly look her in the eye, 'He's not much of a letter writer, but I'm sure I'd hear if the news was bad.'

'So we're all in danger of some sort,' Wendy said, frowning, 'but I wish her messages were clearer.'

Marion licked her lips, 'But we're in danger every day, what with the bombing and everything. And you have your Air Raid Warden work too, Lily. That's dangerous every night. That must be what she meant.'

But it wasn't that simple.

CHAPTER 15

*T*he worst of the Blitz seemed to be over, but we could never relax because there were still occasional bombings. Many people continued to sleep in their Morrison Shelters under their dining table,; others slept in air raid shelters. Air Raid Wardens like me didn't have to face so many awful scenes of death and destruction, but there was still plenty to keep us busy. We made sure people stuck to the black-out rules; helped those who were drunk or lost in the dark find their way home, and call ambulances in emergencies. And we used our local knowledge of shelters and rest centres to find and reunite family members who'd got separated in the rush to find shelter from the bombs. We always had our fingers crossed that their loved ones were unharmed.

Bronwyn had finished her ambulance driver training, and once or twice when I phoned for an ambulance she would be the one to appear. On this Saturday, I was on duty with Marge, a woman about Ruth's age whose children had left home, 'Got to find something to fill my spare time, Dear,' she said, 'can't sit knitting socks or looking at my old man snoring all the time. I'd go potty.'

We did our rounds then went to a Rest Centre to eat our sandwiches. It was busy with WVS volunteers helping homeless families find enough clothes and blankets to see them through. They made us a cup of tea and we sat near a window, glad of the rest. Marge took off her shoes and rubbed her feet, 'I expect I'll break these shoes in one day, but it's taking a lot longer than I expected. I swear my feet are older than the rest of me.'

We'd just finished eating and were folding our sandwich bags when we noticed people stopping and listening. Then we heard it, too. A plane.

There'd been no sirens so we hoped it was one of ours, but experience told us you could never be sure.

Suddenly, there was an enormous swish of bombs falling, and then the Rest Centre shook so much that windows rattled and light fittings hung down from the ceiling ready to fall. Marge hurriedly put her shoes back on as she listened, and we both snatched up our gas masks and first aid kits. A bomb had fallen some way off, opposite the library. One house had had a direct hit.

'Oh, my goodness,' Marge said, 'I hope no-one is in there.'

The houses either side leaned crazily like a child's drawing. We knocked on both doors, relieved to find no-one at home. Nearby houses all had shattered windows.

The road was full of pot holes, flints and lumps of concrete. Water escaped from the mains and mixed with the dust making a sludgy stream that slowly trickled down the road.

Several people were already working with their bare hands to clear the rubble, looking for survivors.

'I think they're out!' someone called, 'I know them, Mr and Mrs Kent. He works at the docks, and she works in an office.'

The rescuers stood up and rubbed their backs, ready to leave the clearing up to the squads whose job it was. But their relief was short lived. A lady ran up from further down the street. She was still in her apron and slippers, and her hair was in rollers, 'She's in! Mrs Kent is in! I saw her go in a few minutes ago. She was wearing a red coat.'

Without pause the volunteers started searching again, throwing aside bricks, wood, broken furniture and household bits and pieces that once made up the home. As they worked a fire started at the back of the house, probably caused by a broken gas pipe.

'Gas!' I shouted, 'Get back! No smoking!'

Marge and I made the onlookers keep their distance; some of them had to be told to move back several times. You'd think they'd know better.

After a quick glance at the fire, the rescuers ignored it and carried on searching. They threw several more household objects aside: a shattered wireless, some books, two saucepans and a frying pan. Five minutes later they found the coat and handed it to me. I brushed it down and laid it on the nearest fence, where the red stood out amongst the dreary grey. Then I carried on helping people nearby who had small injuries from flying debris. Marge paused, cupped her hand to her ear, then nudged me, 'Listen, that's the ambulance! Thank the Lord.' She crossed herself, then continued bandaging a young boy's arm. He yelped and complained as if she were murdering him.

But more was to come.

An unexploded bomb suddenly went off in the next street making us all dive for cover. Tiles, glass, bricks and even an air raid shelter flew over what was left of the roof and we all scattered to avoid getting flattened by flying debris. The noise was phenomenal and the dust got in our eyes and mouths making us choke.

When the worst had passed, we gingerly stood up and shook the dust off our uniforms.

'We'll have to carry on here,' I said to Marge, wiping some grit from my eye, 'someone else will have to deal with that one.'

Then the ambulance arrived and I was glad to see one of the crew was Bronwyn. She and her attendant, an older man, were getting out of the ambulance when the crowd went quiet. Quiet, apart from a dreadful howl which tore into my heart. Mr Kent had arrived a few minutes earlier and frantically joined the search for his wife. His howl was because he'd found her. She was under the kitchen table, lifeless. One side of her head was a mass of blood and gore, and she was covered in brick dust like some ghastly statue.

Without a word two men picked up a door that had been thrown flat and they gently laid her on it; her long wavy brown hair hung over the edge. Bronwyn fetched a blanket from the ambulance and covered her with it, but Mr Kent wouldn't let it cover his wife's face. Even with the dust and blood, he wasn't ready to stop looking at her. He got a handkerchief out of his pocket, dipped it in a puddle of water, wrung it out and tenderly wiped her face. Bronwyn and her attendant waited patiently without saying a word, discreetly wiping a tear away. It was a side of her I'd never seen before. She was usually so blunt, it was a pleasure to see this softness in her.

'I'm not supposed to take the dead in the ambulance,' she whispered to me. 'A special van should take them to the mortuary. But it's like this, I'm here so I'm going to break the rule.'

I squeezed her arm, 'I'm glad it's you.'

The men loaded Mrs Kent into the back of the ambulance. 'Can I go with her?' Mr Kent asked.

'We'll be going to the mortuary. Do you feel up to that? It's not a great place to be.'

He nodded, holding back tears, 'I'll hold her hand all the way there.'

Bronwyn helped him in the back ,then came forward to get in the driver's seat. 'I hope someone will love me that much one day.' she said.

CHAPTER 16

*N*ext morning Ruth was late for work and when she arrived she had deep shadows under her eyes.

'Sorry, sorry,' she said, taking off her coat, 'I'm fit for nothing today. I've been up most of the night. Nudge me awake if I nod off.'

Marion turned to her, 'What happened then? Why didn't you get any sleep?'

Ruth sat at her desk and took the cover off her typewriter, 'I was on WVS duty for the evening, but we got a call to say that one of the other Rest Centres had collapsed. Apparently a bomb dropped nearby a few days ago but they thought it was okay. It turns out it wasn't.'

We looked at Mr Lynch wondering if he'd moan about us chatting, but instead he asked, 'What did you have to do, Ruth?'

'Some of us went over there and set up a mobile canteen to provide refreshments for the clear-up squad and anyone else who needed it. Thank goodness no-one was seriously hurt. They heard the building creaking and ran out. But all their equipment was ruined, not to mention all the donated clothes and household stuff.'

'See how you get on today,' Mr Lynch said, 'if it's too much let me know and I'll fix it so you can go home early.'

He left the room and we stared at the door with our mouths open.

'Wow!' Edith said, 'never known him to take so much notice of anything we say, much less be so kind.' she turned to Ruth, 'who looked after your kids?'

Ruth was winding paper into her machine, 'I managed to get a message to the baby-sitter and she stayed the night, bless her heart. I often wish I had a live-in baby-sitter. That'd solve a lot of problems.'

'I'm going to the Ladies,' Marion said, pushing back her chair. I noticed Ruth frown as she looked at her.

'It's not my place to ask,' she said when Marion left the room, 'but is Marion in the family way? I thought she was just putting on weight but now I'm not so sure. I thought she wasn't married.'

Bronwyn and I looked at each other, 'I think you'd better ask her,' I said, 'it's not up to me to say.'

Ten minutes later Mr Lynch came back in, 'Okay girls, time for your break. Be back in fifteen minutes!'

We went to our grandly named Staff Room. In reality it was an unused room full of cast-off bits and pieces of furniture. Four ancient brown threadbare chairs lined up against one wall, and two stained blue, typing chairs faced them.

Ruth and Marion were together putting on the kettle and getting out the cups and the big brown tea-pot. I could just make out their conversation.

Ruth was spooning tea leaves into the pot, not looking at

Marion, 'Marion, I'm really sorry if I've got the wrong end of the stick but are you... well... are you...'

Marion stopped what she was doing, 'Expecting a baby?' she sighed, 'yes. And before you ask, no, my boyfriend isn't going to make an honest woman of me.'

Ruth dropped her voice, 'That's terrible. You poor thing. Don't tell anyone outside this room, but that happened to my sister. She found out too late that her boyfriend was already married. She was in a terrible state.'

'Blimey, what happened?'

The kettle whistled and Ruth poured the water into the teapot. 'My family is very strict about that sort of thing and worried she'd bring disgrace on us all. They made her go to a mother-and-baby home in Scotland. They'd have sent her to the other end of the world if they could. They made her leave before she even showed. She was so upset, she couldn't stop crying.'

She stirred the tea leaves and put everything on a tray. 'She had to give the baby up for adoption.' Her voice cracked as she spoke, 'They found a good Jewish family, but it still broke her heart. I love my parents, they are good people, but they set too much store by what other people think. If my daughter had that problem I'd never turn her out, no matter what the neighbours might say!'

I'd been nearest to them and Edith and Bronwyn were chatting about something else so I pretended not to have heard.

'Hey, Bronwyn, you've got a date tonight,' I said when there was a pause in the conversation. 'Where are you going?'

'And who with?' Edith said, all ears.

Bronwyn tapped the side of her nose. 'That's for me to know,' she said with a grin, 'and I'm not sure where we're going, but it'll be somewhere swanky. Better wear my last pair of decent stockings.'

'Make the most of it,' Edith said, 'dating is the best part of a relationship, that's what I say.'

In the past she'd always talked about her Sidney lovingly, but since he got back from the war she often dropped hints that things weren't going well. As far as I knew I was the only one she'd spoken to about it, so I didn't say more.

It turned out I didn't need to.

We'd just returned to our desks and started typing again when the door opened with such force it banged against the wall. We all stopped typing and looked up.

To our surprise Sidney walked in, his steps unsteady. He looked as if he hadn't long got out of bed; his hair was sticking up all over the place, he had odd socks on and he looked unfocussed.

'Edith?' he mumbled, without registering her properly. He staggered over to Edith who had jumped out of her chair. Mr Lynch stood up too, looking bemused, 'Who is this, Edith?' he asked, 'is he drunk?' I caught his eye and shook my head.

Edith went to Sidney and put her arm round his shoulders. 'It's okay, Sidney, I'm here, I'm here.' she turned to Mr Lynch, 'I'm really sorry, but I'll have to take him home. He's not well. I'll be back later or tomorrow.'

'I'll stay late and make up your work,' Ruth said.

'Me too,' the rest of us said, 'between us it won't take too long.'

She covered her typewriter, picked up her things, then threaded her arm through Sidney's. 'You can explain,' she said to me as she guided her flustered husband out of the door.

When she'd gone the others looked at me questioningly.

'You know he had a head injury,' I said, 'he's still recovering and it will take a while.' I saw no reason to go into more detail, although Ruth plied me with questions. I felt such sadness for Edith. It seemed that Sidney was more poorly than I had understood. I could only offer her my support and pray that he would return to the man he had once been.

CHAPTER 17

J sat looking at the dockets, a deep frown on my forehead. Our depot supplied a wide range of goods to the army, so it was no surprise if we got returns from time to time. But I started to notice a pattern. Among other mundane items like tinned corned beef, we supplied weapons and army uniforms, but had received more than usual returns for two items: Enfield guns and soldiers' boots. It was a strange combination and that convinced me I must be mistaken. I kept looking through the paperwork sure I was missing something.

It was a hot day and the paper stuck to my sweaty hands as I rifled through the pile of papers. There was no clear pattern. There wasn't a return every tenth consignment or anything. That made me doubt myself even more. At random I chose something else we supplied; another type of gun. There were far fewer returns for those; only about a quarter of the number. Then I looked at soldiers' belts; hardly any returns. Caps; none at all. So although we weren't talking about big numbers, they were big by comparison to everything else. I sat back in my chair and bit my thumb nail. I'd been right once before when I spotted a discrepancy, but that didn't make me right this time.

My mind ran through the possibilities. I might be reading the figures wrong; numbers have never been my strong point. The staff who took in the returns could have entered them wrong. Or perhaps it was a coincidence.

I needed someone to check them with me before I took any further action.

~

'What do you think, Bronwyn?' I said, looking over her shoulder at the figures I'd jotted down earlier. I'd probably get in a lot of trouble if Mr McDonald or Mr Lynch knew I'd taken them home. We weren't supposed to 'leak' anything out of the Depot, but Bronwyn worked in the same place so I risked it. I didn't want anyone else to know in case I was imagining things, so I'd waited until we were both home the same evening and Marion was out.

Bronwyn ran her finger down the list of figures, 'What sort of problems are they reporting?'

'Guns not firing, soles coming off boots far too soon, that sort of thing. Both of them can put a soldier's life in danger.'

She let out a low whistle. 'These figures by yere are serious, not huge numbers but definitely enough to make me suspicious,' she said, tapping the piece of paper, 'who supplied this stuff?'

I pursed my lips, 'Biggerstaff. The guy you thought was lush.'

She sat back in her chair as if she'd been pushed without warning, 'Biggerstaff?'

'Yep. You certainly know how to pick them.'

135

She bristled, 'Hey, not so much of that. Anyroad, I've never been out with him. He's asked me a couple of times, mind, but I stuck to my guns. No married men. You suggesting all my blokes have been crooks?

I raised an eyebrow, which she ignored.

'You'll tell Mr McDonald about this, won't you?'

We heard Wendy coming down the stairs so I grabbed the paper from Bronwyn and shoved it in my bag, 'I'm going to do some more checking first,' I whispered a second before Wendy knocked.

'Can I come in?' she asked, poking her head round the door. We only locked it when we went to bed. As usual, she looked immaculate, this time in a blue and white gathered dress with a white cardigan over the top. There was a shadow of a bruise on her jaw.

'Of course, come in. Want a cuppa?'

She took a couple of steps into the room and, with a flourish, held out a bottle she'd been hiding behind her back.

'It's port, almost full,' she said, looking like a naughty schoolgirl, 'it's Thomas's, but he's away for a few days so I'll have time to replace it.'

Knowing his temper, I hoped she managed to find the same brand before he came back. We fetched our small assortment of mismatched glasses, and poured ourselves a generous measure of the sticky dark red drink. My first sip made me cough, but it warmed my chest and I soon took a second.

Wendy held up her glass, 'Cheers, Girls.' She turned the glass round, inspecting the chip on one side, 'My mother-in-law would be horrified if she saw me now. She only drinks port out of special glasses and only at a given time each evening. Regular as clockwork she is, and not just her bowels.' she giggled and I wondered if she'd already been at the booze.

'Sounds like she's a creature of habit,' Bronwyn said with a grin.

Wendy wiped her mouth, 'You're not kidding. Everything is regimented. Towels have to be hung exactly level; washing up done in a certain order; front door step scrubbed every morning at seven; special crockery and cutlery for each meal and for guests,' she sighed, 'I suppose that's where Thomas gets his funny little ways from.'

'What funny ways are those?' I asked.

She gave a bitter laugh, 'Oh, just little things. Like his mother I suppose. Likes things just so, keeps me on my toes. You have to be a good housewife, don't you!'

I looked around and wondered what she made of our place. It was clean, but no-one would say everything was in its place. My shoes were where I kicked them off, a cardigan was on the back of a chair, a dirty cup was on the floor and two newspapers and a book were next to my chair. And we hadn't dusted for at least two weeks.

'And he doesn't like me disagreeing with him,' she added, 'but then he knows so much more than me. I should learn from him rather than argue.'

Bronwyn and I had many times discussed whether we should let Wendy know what we heard when they rowed. Many people said you shouldn't interfere in what goes on between a man and his wife, but it was hard to ignore. Especially when we saw another bruise or heard a thump and a muffled scream.

'Battering the old woman was pretty common when I was growing up,' Bronwyn said when we were talking about it, 'the blokes who didn't were called angels. Says something doesn't it, that a kind man is considered an angel. They should be considered normal if you ask me.'

'My dad was handy as well, but his was mostly the occasional swipe rather than real battering.'

In the end we decided we'd mention it to Wendy if a suitable opportunity came up.

This was it.

We looked at each other, 'Not being funny nor nothing,' Bronwyn said, 'but we can hear some of what goes on upstairs,' she nodded towards the ceiling, 'it doesn't sound a bit funny. Sounds like you have a rough time up there.'

Wendy froze, eyes darting from side to side as if she was seeking an escape route. 'Well, it's... it's not... not what it seems.'

We both waited for her to continue, but she looked into her glass then took another sip of her port. I wondered what was going through her mind. She could make up a story to explain the noises we heard, although it was difficult to imagine what that might be. She was probably too embarrassed realising we knew her predicament. Or maybe her mind was so scrambled she didn't know how to respond. I felt sorry for her and wanted to put my arms round her, but didn't feel we knew each other well enough. My muscles tensed as I waited for her to answer.

The silence lengthened so eventually I spoke, 'If it's not what it seems, what is it? I'm sorry if we seem nosy, but we've been worried about you.'

'You don't have to tell us if you don't want to,' Bronwyn added.

'It'll work out,' Wendy said without looking up, 'my mother always said if you're a good enough wife, you'll have a good husband. He just needs my help to sort himself out.'

Bronwyn choked on her mouthful of port, spitting it all

down her top. She ran into the kitchen and got a damp cloth to wipe herself with. 'My granny,' she said when she'd finished, 'God rest her annoying soul, rarely said anything useful. She was usually too drunk. But she once gave me some good advice.'

Wendy looked up, 'What was that, then?'

'Never marry a man to fix him. If he needs fixing when you meet him, he'll always need fixing unless he does something about it himself. She told me she'd married my granddad thinking she'd help him. He never changed no matter how hard she tried.'

There was silence for a minute, then Wendy muttered into her glass, 'I can help him. I can.'

She put her glass down on the floor and stood up, 'Excuse me, Girls, I've got a bit of a headache. I think I'll have an early night.' She picked up the nearly empty port bottle, gave a half-hearted smile and left.

Wendy's husband returned home three days later. I swear the atmosphere changed in the whole house as soon as he set foot inside the door. It was like he had some nasty germ that swirled round the house instantly floating in the air somehow.

He slammed the front door and banged on our door as he walked past. I hurried to open it, but he was already half way up the stairs and didn't even turn round when I called his name.

Half an hour later we heard the familiar sounds of an argument - a crash and sudden silence.

'I'm never getting married,' Marion said, 'I don't know a single good man.'

'I do,' I said, 'my manager at the picture house is good, and a lot of the ARP men. Mr Lynch's a drip, but he's not a bad man. Mr McDonald is okay too. There's plenty of good ones, it's just a matter of finding them.' *Edward's a good man.* The thought popped into my head, but I was still too angry with him to accept it.

Marion's shoulders slumped, 'No-one's going to want me once they know I've already had a kiddie.'

Bronwyn was tidying the room as we spoke, 'You going to tell them then? Is it any of their business, what happened before you met them?'

Marion's cheeks went pink, 'Well, he'll know I've... you know... on our wedding night, won't he?'

I leaned over and put my hand on her arm, 'A good friend of mine who's a nurse said you can't tell. Us girls are all different and how our bodies react our first time is different, too.'

She looked up, 'Is that for real?'

'It is. You might think now you'll never want to get married and have more children, but I bet you'll change your mind when the pain of losing this one is not so bad.'

Bronwyn put some newspapers near the fireplace. 'She's right, you know,' she said, 'but let me tell you another bit of my granny's advice. Wow, tidy, that's two pieces of advice she gave me. Pity she didn't act on them herself, she got a real useless dab of a husband.'

'What was the other bit of advice, then?' I asked.

'She said listen to how your boyfriend talks to and about other people. If he's always rude or sort of negative about people, run a mile. That's what she said. Run a mile. 'Cos when he's over the first flush of love, or lust as she called it, it's you who'll cop all that negative stuff. Makes sense, doesn't it.'

The door upstairs slammed and Wendy's husband's boots thundered down the stairs. Without warning our door was thrown open making us jump. We were all so startled we stood up without saying a word.

He, I had to struggle to remember his name, Thomas, stood there looking ready to kill. His fists were clenched and his face was so red I thought he's have a stroke or a heart attack any minute. He'd changed out of his officer's uniform and was wearing brown corduroy trousers and a cream shirt. No tie. You'd think that would make a man look more human, but not him. He stood, legs apart, feet firmly planted on the floor, and glared at the three of us as if we'd done something wrong.

'Can I help you?' I asked.

He put his hands on his hips, 'YOU!' he shouted at me, 'Can keep your mouth shut. And YOU...' he pointed to Marion, 'shouldn't be here. I've checked and this flat is only for two people. Your name isn't on the lease. You... should... not ... be... here... You've got twelve hours to get out. Got it?'

We stood with our mouths open, too stunned to reply.

'I said, GOT IT?' he pointed at Marion again, 'YOU! OUT! Or the Military police will be here tomorrow to throw you and that bastard you're carrying out.'

He spun on his heels and stormed back out the door, slamming it so hard behind him, it's a wonder it didn't fall off its hinges.

It was as if the air had been sucked out of the room. We were left gasping for breath. A pause and then we all fell into our chairs; our legs having lost their strength.

Marion looked at her watch. 'Can he do that?' she whispered, 'It's eight o'clock. Twelve hours is eight o'clock tomorrow morning. Where can I go?'

We spend ages talking over the possibilities, but all of

them were rejected by Marion for one reason or other. Her brothers and sisters either wouldn't or couldn't help. Her father definitely wouldn't, and her mother was too weak to stand up to him. Friends had their own problems; they'd been bombed or had no spare rooms. Marion's shoulders dropped lower and lower as we spoke, 'It's hopeless.' she said, wiping a tear from her cheek.

We were silent for a couple of minutes, then Bronwyn piped up, 'How about next door? They're easy going and didn't ask too many questions about where your husband was.'

Marion put her hand to her heart, 'I couldn't ask them, I've only met them the once. It wouldn't be fair.'

Bronwyn leapt out of her seat, 'Wait a minute.' she said, and walked out of the flat without another word. We heard the front door open and close.

'What's she doing?' Marion asked, 'she's not asking them, is she?'

I didn't know, but it was the type of thing Bronwyn would do. She'd say, with good reason, they could always say no if they wanted to.

Marion sat wringing her hands, apologising again and again for putting us in this awkward position. No amount of reassurance would make her feel better.

Less than ten minutes later Bronwyn bounced back in, eager as a puppy, her smile a mile wide. 'It's all sorted,' she said, 'give them an hour to get the bed made and you can move in, or move in tomorrow morning. Up to you.'

After a second's pause Marion stood up and hugged her so tight she had to plead for breath, 'Oh, thank you, thank you,' she said over and over again. 'They're lovely people, and I'll be right next door to you.'

'Hey!', Bronwyn said, taking half a step back, 'you hugged me so hard I felt your baby kick!'

Marion smiled, 'Yes, he's a lively one,' her smile faded, 'pity I won't see him growing up. I just hope he has good parents who'll give him as much love as I would.' She made an excuse and went into the bedroom closing the door behind her.

CHAPTER 18

J don't know what I'm going to do,' Edith said, 'in some ways Sidney's a bit better. He has moments when he's his old self, but then he just sort of switches off.'

For once, Edith and I were the only ones having our dinner break together. We walked along the quietest street near the Depot, eating our sandwiches as we went. I tried to imagine having her life. Working and looking after a poorly husband. The life she thought she'd have turned into something close to a nightmare.

I took my cheese sandwich out of its bag, 'What do the doctors say?'

A horse and cart went by, the clip-clopping of the hooves and the shouts of 'giddy up, horse' drowning our words for a minute.

'The doctors don't really know. They say it's a good sign if he has a few moments back to normal now and then. They hope he'll gradually get better,' she folded up her paper sandwich bag and put it in her handbag, 'it's so lovely when he's his old self. I cling on to those moments when I feel drowning in despair. But the... you know... the other business, well, that's the same and the doctors don't think it will get any better now.'

I turned to her, 'You mean in bed?' I kept my voice low because people were walking by.

She nodded, 'You won't tell anyone will you, but I miss it. I suppose I'd got used to not... well, you know... while he was away with the army. Now we can have a cuddle, I want more. It doesn't look as if it'll happen though.'

'I'm so sorry,' I said, wishing I had a magic wand to make things right for her, 'life's been very unfair to you, especially when you want a family.'

She shrugged as if it were nothing, but her face gave away her true feelings, 'I shouldn't complain. A lot of people have worse, much worse. He might have died or lost a leg or something.'

'But other people having it worse doesn't make your problem any less real,' I said, 'it still hurts just as much.'

'Let's talk about something else before I get all gloomy,' she said, 'how's Marion getting on with your neighbours? I forgot to ask her.'

We walked around some sandbags, then crossed the road to walk back to the Depot a different way. 'She comes with me and Bronwyn to work in the morning, but because of our war work we haven't seen her often in the evening. She seems okay, though. They're a strange lot, but you've got to like them.'

'What do they do for a living? You never said.'

'That's the funny thing, Marion said they don't seem to have a job, any of them. Perhaps they inherited money. They seem to spend most of their time drinking and smoking weird smelling cigarettes.'

'I wish I'd known she was looking for somewhere to live,' she said, 'we've got a spare room and I wouldn't mind some help with the rent. It'd cheer Sydney up having someone else to talk to as well as me.'

A car nearby backfired, making us jump. After so much bombing we were all living on our nerves, even if we did talk about being brave and having the famous Blighty spirit.

'Why don't you tell Marion.' I suggested, 'it would be good for her to have a backup and better for you than having a lodger you don't know. Would your neighbours say anything about her being in the family way?'

We stopped and looked both ways before crossing the road, 'You sorted that out with saying her husband is away at war. It's so common I don't think anyone would think twice about it. Anyway, it can't be that long before she goes to the mother-and-baby home.'

That evening I was alone at home. Marion was next door and Bronwyn was on ATS ambulance duty. I fried up a bit of left over mashed potato and cabbage and put a fried egg on top. I mopped up the juices with a chunk of grey bread - the quality of bread got worse every day.

I ate the scrappy meal on my knee and settled down to read a book I'd got from the library. It was *For whom the Bell Tolls* by Ernest Hemingway, about a volunteer attached to a guerrilla unit during the Spanish Civil War. Rumour had it that the Brits had spies doing the type of work he did in France, blowing up bridges and important buildings. I put the book down, wondering how you'd get into being a spy or guerilla. It had to be dangerous work, even more dangerous than being on Air Raid Protection duty during the worst of the bombing. After the stint Bronwyn and I did in Paris, my French was pretty good. I'd got round having an accent by saying I was Dutch. No-one ever queried it; France is such a big country people in different regions had different accents anyway. I guessed the powers-that-be would have to give you proper training. It sounded exciting, a lot different from paperwork at the Depot.

Lost in thought I didn't hear the door bell first time, but the sound of Wendy clattering down the stairs at the second ring bought me out of my daydream. We reached the door at the same time.

She opened it and let out a little squeal. It was a young lad, a messenger boy in his bike gear, goggles pushed to the top of his head. He couldn't have been older than fourteen. His young unlined face was mournful, mouth turned down at the corners. The lads were called the angels of death because they so often delivered the worst type of news.

It was pouring and the boy and his bike were dripping wet. An ambulance went by, its siren shattering our frozen minds. The dreaded envelope he was holding was soggy despite his attempts to keep it dry.

'Who's it for?' I asked, my voice shaking. *Please*, I was silently praying, *don't let it be Edward.*

'Telegram for Mrs Archer,' he said, looking from one to the other of us. My knees wobbled with relief and for a second I leaned against the wall, but quickly came to my senses. My relief was spoiled by the bad news Wendy was about to receive.

'Who is it?' she asked the lad. He knew without her saying that she was asking who was dead.

'Sorry Mrs Archer, I don't know. We're not allowed to open the telegrams.'

Wendy didn't try to take it from his hand, so holding her

arm with one hand, I took it from him. I nodded my thanks, and he turned round and hurried away.

'Come in with me,' I said, guiding her into our rooms. She hadn't said a word and looked around her without seeing anything, her face so pale I thought she might faint.

I sat her in a chair and put a blanket over her knees. She was shaking so much her knees moved the blanket up and down. I knelt on the floor in front of her, saying nothing, waiting for her to be ready to speak. She sat, eyes squeezed shut, hand on her heart, her breathing shallow. Eventually she asked, 'Will you open it, Lily? Tell me who it is. My brother is in France somewhere. It can't be Thomas, he's in this country somewhere.'

'Are you sure you want me to open it?'

She nodded, 'You do it. I'll never be brave enough.'

I sat back on my heels and tore open the envelope, my heart thumping. Sometimes the news wasn't too awful, I knew that from experience, but often it was the worst news imaginable.

The telegram said,

'I deeply regret to inform you that your husband, Major
Thomas Archer,
has died of a heart attack.
The army express their profound sympathy.
Letter confirming this telegram follows.'

I read it to her, but she didn't take it in and I had to read it a second time.

Without a word she reached out her hand and took it from me, turning it over and over, inspecting it as if I'd made a mistake.

She looked up, 'Not killed in action. Heart attack.'

I leaned forward and held her hand, 'Poor you. Poor Thomas. It will have been quick, I hope that's a consolation.'

She gave a harsh sound that might have been a laugh, 'How he'd have hated that, the indignity of dying that way. A battlefield death would be more his style.'

Finally, she gave way and tears fell. But before I could say anything else the doorbell rang again. We jumped as if a firing pistol had been shot in the room.

'It isn't... not another one...' she whispered, 'my brother...'

'Stay there!' I ordered, and walked to the door on wobbly legs.

It was Marion, standing under an umbrella, her coat thrown over her shoulders and still wearing her bedroom slippers. Her face was sombre.

'I heard,' she said, 'the telegram boys always tell a neighbour.'

I pulled her inside. 'She's in here. It's Thomas. Heart attack. She's still taking it in, I think.'

We went into our living room. Wendy looked up, fear in her eyes.

'It wasn't another telegram, it's Marion. The messenger boy told her you'd had a telegram.'

'Would you like me to stay?' Marion asked, 'I'll go back if you'd rather.'

Wendy shook her head, and Marion went to sit next to her.

'We don't have any port,' I said, 'but a sweet tea is good for shock they say. I'll put the kettle on.'

The rain battered the kitchen window, and trees in the garden were knocked around in all directions as if it were winter. I shivered and put my hands near the gas cooker to warm myself. As I waited for the kettle to boil I remembered the message the fortune teller had given Wendy, 'You'll have bad news, and it will be the best news you can ever have.' Or words to that effect. I put the cups and saucers on a tray and poured the boiling water into the teapot, giving the leaves a stir. Maybe, once she'd got over the shock, Wendy would be glad to be free of her violent husband and be able to start her life again. But it was too soon to say that to her.

Back in the room Wendy and Marion were talking in low voices. I put down the tray and began pouring the tea. Marion opened her bag and took out a bottle of sherry.

'When Vanessa heard what had happened she gave me this. Have we got enough glasses?'

'Tea and sherry?' I said, 'Well, why not?'

We were silent as I poured the drinks. For a few minutes we talked about other things. I'd noticed in the past that it's sometimes as if the brain can't keep focussed on horror. It dips in and out of thinking about something else, then comes back to reality.

Wendy left her tea and drank her sherry in one long swig. She coughed and wiped her mouth with her hanky. 'Can I have another?' she said.

She held the refilled glass in the air, 'Let's drink a toast to Thomas, God rest his soul.'

We clinked glasses, each lost in our own thoughts.

'How will I manage without him?' Wendy said, sobbing again, 'he did everything. I don't even know how to write a cheque. I'll be lost without him.'

I waited until her sobs subsided a little. 'What did you do before you met Thomas?'

'I was a secretary for a solicitor.'

'Then you must have a lot of experience to call on. Secretaries have heaps of skills. I know it's hard to take in at the moment, but you might surprise yourself by how quickly you pick all that stuff up.'

For a moment she had a spark of hope in her eyes. 'Do you think so?' then the tears started again, 'but I'm nothing without Thomas.'

We let her go over and over the awfulness of losing her husband, rehearsing how dreadful her life would be. A hundred times I wanted to contradict the things she said about her being a hopeless woman.

'You know we'll help you with anything,' I said, 'arranging the funeral or anything else.'

'Oh my word, the funeral! There'll be loads to do. I have no idea where to start.'

'I think you have to go to the Registrar's office to register his death. I can find out by tomorrow and let you know. I'll come with you if you like.'

She gave a watery smile, 'There's one good thing. Once the funeral is over, I'll never have to see that old witch of a mother of his!'

Over the course of an hour her attitude gradually changed to a state where she could see that she might feel better one day.

'I'm Catholic,' she said out of nowhere, 'Catholics are married for ever. For better or worse. I had to make it work.'

Until death do us part, I thought. I should have been feeling sorry for Thomas, but wasn't able to bring myself to do that yet.

'What will you do?' Marion asked after a while.

'Do you mean now? I'll have to move out, this is an army hiring.'

'I don't suppose they'll make you move out immediately,' I said, 'they'll probably give you plenty of time to sort things out.'

She rubbed her chin, 'I'll go to my sister's. I can stay with her for a while.'

It was a ray of hope; the beginning of her thinking about the rest of her life. She would have a lot of memories to think through; a lot of Thomas's behaviour and her own to sort out in her head.

CHAPTER 19

*N*ow Bronwyn had confirmed my thoughts that the discrepancies in returns weren't my imagination, I felt more confident about taking action. Two soldiers always guarded the warehouse where guns and ammunition were stored. I'd passed the time of day with them as I walked around, but unlike the men who worked in the depot, they changed regularly so I didn't know any of them well.

I did my usual rounds, then went to speak to them. They both stepped forward, looking pleased to have a break from the monotony of standing outside a warehouse all day.

'Can we help you, Sweetheart?' the taller one asked. His uniform trousers didn't quite reach his shoes and showed a couple of inches of sock, giving him a comical look. The other one was shorter, medium height and had a round face with a nasty scar down one cheek.

'Do you have a minute?' I said, 'I have a query about returns.'

'Don't know anything about that,' scarface said, 'we don't deal with that sort of stuff. We just make sure no-one nicks anything.'

'I know,' I said, 'but I have a question.'

'Go on then, Doll, what is it?' the tall one asked. I wanted to hit him. I'm not a doll, I'm a soldier just like him.

I took a deep breath to keep my temper, 'Have either of you been in action?'

Scarface nodded, 'I have. Why d'you ask?'

'We supply Enfield guns. Have you ever used them?'

He laughed like I was the most stupid person in the world, 'Every soldier who's been in action has used them.' It was clearly a dig and me and the tall one.

'How often would you expect to get a faulty one?'

He frowned, 'A faulty gun? Is that what you mean?'

I nodded, 'If one was faulty would you know straight away or do they go wrong after a bit of use?'

He took off his cap and scratched his head, 'Let me think. They can get clogged up with mud and stuff. The barrel can get damaged. The pin could fall out. That the sort of thing you mean?'

'Yes, how often does that happen?'

He put his cap back on, 'Mostly they don't go wrong at all, but sometimes they get bunged up with all sorts. That's why they give us so much training on how to clean them, even in the dark.'

'So you don't have much trouble with the barrels?'

He laughed, 'Only when a tank rolls over them on hard ground. What d'you want to know for, anyway?'

I dodged his question, 'What about boots? D'you often have trouble with them?'

The tall one joined in the conversation, 'Are you kidding? Trouble with boots? We've all got blisters to prove the trouble. How come they never fit properly, that's what I'd like to know.'

I thought about my own boots; women soldiers had all the same problems. 'What about the soles falling off?'

They looked at each other, and scarface spoke, 'After a lot of use they can fall apart just like any other boots. And I heard that in North Africa they're having that problem. The heat melts the glue or something.'

'But not anywhere else?'

'Not that I'm aware of, but it can get hot anywhere sometimes, can't it? Come on, what's this all about? You don't think there's something dodgy going on, do you? You got nothing better to do sitting there in that comfy office?'

'Yeah,' the tall one said, 'not on your little feet all day like we are. You're making up problems where there ain't any. Filling your pretty little head with nonsense, that's what you're doing. Fancy coming out some time?'

I ignored that, thanked them and went back to my desk. Was I making something out of nothing? I didn't want to bother Mr McDonald until I had more to go on, but I didn't know how to get more evidence.

I'd have to get creative.

I didn't know what I was getting myself in to.

~

The answer to my problem came sooner than I expected.

It was the next morning, a day full of fluffy white clouds, with blue sky peeking through, promising a sunny day later. There was a query about a consignment of Corned Beef, so clutching the relevant paperwork I strolled over to one of the warehouses. It was the one where Ruth had seen the Swastika symbol. One man was busy loading a lorry and another unloading pallets of goods the lorry had just dropped off. While they were busy, I went to the post and saw the Swastika had been scribbled over. I hoped that meant someone spotted it and didn't like it. But it might have meant the supervisor saw it and made them remove it.

I walked up the stairs to the Supervisor's office. It was a small room with flimsy walls, just big enough to hold a desk, two chairs and one filing cabinet. A calendar was on the wall along with a *Careless Talk Costs Lives* poster.

We soon sorted out the issue, and I headed back down the stairs where Mr Biggerstaff was talking to Jimmy, one of the warehouse men. I'd seen them together a few times. There was probably an innocent explanation, but perhaps it was something more sinister.

When they saw me they stopped talking as suddenly as if I'd put a magic spell on them. Jimmy said goodbye, and walked towards another lorry that had just arrived.

～

That evening Bronwyn and I were on our way to see *We'll smile again* with Flanagan and Allen; it promised to be a good laugh.

'How's your ARP work going?' Bronwyn asked, pulling me across the road when there was a small gap in the traffic.

'Not so frantic now we're not bombed every night, but we still have to make sure everyone gets their blackout done. If I had a penny for every time someone swore at me or called me Mrs Hitler for reminding them to cover their lights, I'd be rich. At least we have time for a bit of a rest now. What about you?'

'Same as you, I suppose. Bombings might not be so often, but you wouldn't believe how many people fall into holes, or over sandbags, or whatever in the dark and break bones.

156

Doesn't help if they're blind drunk, of course. Mind you, at least the booze anaesthetises them,' she paused, 'something dreadful happened last time I was on duty and bombs dropped.'

'What was that?'

She walked slowly; slumped, heavy footed.

'We got called to a street, and it turned out to be where the man on duty with me lived. He was frantic as we drove there, almost jumping up and down in his seat at every detour we had to take. I was so scared for him I could hardly drive straight.'

'What happened?'

She took a deep breath, 'The house next to his took a direct hit. That was bad enough because he and his wife were friends of theirs. But his house was mostly collapsed too; half of upstairs had fallen in. There'd been no siren, so he worried his wife and baby were at home, not in the shelter.'

My breath caught in my throat, 'Oh, my goodness. Were they?'

'We had to stop him rushing into what was left of the house. It was obviously unsafe. Luckily the rescue squad came a minute later, and they went in. He ran in with them even though we told him not to. He went crazy trying to clear away the debris,' she paused again and swallowed hard, 'they were both dead. His wife had been bathing the baby by the fire and the blast threw the baby into the fire. He came out carrying this poor burnt baby. He was still recognisable, but bits of him were burnt to a cinder. Poor little chap. We've seen so much horror, but that was the worst. Absolutely the worst. I had trouble not throwing up, and I've dreamt about it every night since.'

My chest ached as I listened to her, and I held her hand and waited for her to carry on.

'Well, he insisted on going to the mortuary with the baby and his wife. She didn't get burnt, but part of the upper floor had fallen on her. You can imagine what state she was in. We drove him and the bodies to the mortuary, but he wouldn't let us go in with him. I haven't seen him since. Poor, poor man. Will this damn war never end?'

Every ambulance driver or ARP warden had dreadful stories to tell; events that kept us awake at night and would live with us for ever.

We walked without speaking for a while, arm in arm. It was a bomber's moon, so we easily saw ahead of us. There was a lot of action around a nearby church; two police cars and several policemen as well as a crowd watching.

The church had been bombed a while before, although half of it still stood; dangerous to anyone brave enough to go in. Yet that's what the police were doing.

'What's going on?' I asked one of the bystanders.

Before she answered an ambulance pulled up, and two ARP men jumped out. 'I know one of them,' Bronwyn said and hurried over to speak to him. I followed her.

'What's going on?' she asked.

'A body,' the man said. Finding bodies in bombed buildings was nothing unusual. Rescuers did their best and usually found people, dead or alive, but it was always possible to miss someone, especially if the building was unsafe.

Her friend excused himself and went into the church. 'Let me know if I can do anything,' Bronwyn called after him.

The police were moving a slab in a side chapel. Only one wall remained, and it looked like a strong gust of wind would make it fall over and flatten them.

'What on earth are they doing?' I wondered, 'surely that slab has been there for ever.'

Half an hour later Bronwyn's friend came over to us, 'A

murder.' he said, 'got to be. Someone cut the woman's arms and legs off.'

'I wonder how many murders are disguised as bomb injuries,' Bronwyn said, 'but most of the murderers must be a bit brighter than whoever did that.'

CHAPTER 20

a frantic knock at the door made me jump; my heart in my mouth. I'd only been home for half an hour and was looking forward to a rare night in. It was all planned; corned beef hash for tea and a night listening to the radio and knitting a scarf. Despite Bronwyn trying to teach me how to knit, a scarf was about the limit of my skills.

The knocking reminded me of the time the lad came with the awful telegram for Wendy. I walked to the door, mentally checking off who might be dead or injured; my mum, Edward, Bronwyn's mum. So it was a huge relief when I saw Marion there, even if she did look fraught. She was carrying a suitcase, and had a bag over her shoulder.

'They're gone!' she cried, 'they've only bloody done a runner. Can I come in?'

Baffled, I stood aside and let her in, taking the case from her. She sat down heavily in our tatty armchair and put her head in her hands.

'Who's gone?' I asked sitting opposite her.

'Vanessa and all of them next door. Gone. The place is completely empty, like they've never been there.'

'You mean they've moved out? Didn't they warn you?'

'Not a word, nothing. I let myself in like I usually do, and there was my case and bag in the hall. I couldn't make head nor tail of it. I thought I must have done something to annoy them. The living room was empty as a barn. Stripped bare, every last thing gone.'

'Was the rest of the house empty, too?'

She nodded, 'Just bits and pieces of rubbish, but it's like they never lived there. I'm furious. Got a cuppa? I'm parched. I don't know what I'm going to do. Can I stay here at least tonight?'

I walked towards the kitchen to put the kettle on the gas, 'Of course you can, but I told you we've had word not to have other people staying. Not to worry, we'll sort something out.'

I got the cups and saucers on a tray, and got out the acorn coffee. While I waited for the kettle to boil, I went back in to chat to her. 'Any idea why Vanessa left? She seemed such a lovely person.'

She twisted the ring on her finger. 'I suppose it was good she packed up my stuff. But I think they hadn't paid the rent for ages.'

The kettle whistled and I headed for the kitchen, remembering that Amanda said they often moved. Maybe that was why. Wait until the bailiffs appeared or court action was threatened and then high-tail it.

'How do you know about the rent?' I asked.

'Little things I overheard, but I paid them my share so I didn't take much notice to be honest.'

I laughed, 'They've got some cheek, taking rent off you but not paying it to the landlord. Blimey O'Riley.'

She stifled a laugh, 'I hadn't thought of that. Go on, get that coffee poured. Do you have any ideas where I can go?

It's not for long, I'll soon be going to Colchester, worst luck.'

I handed her a cup, 'It's like this. Me and Edith were talking about you a while ago and she said she'd be willing to put you up.'

Her eyes opened wide, 'Really? She said that? But what about Sidney? Is he better?'

'He's getting better slowly. You'd better ask her, but I think she reckons having someone else in the house would be good for him. You can help look after him too, I suppose.'

'Gosh, that would be such a load off my mind. I'll ask her in the morning. I'm waiting for Mr Lynch to notice, and tell me I've got to leave. He must go round with his eyes closed.'

In fact, I'd seen him looking at her stomach a few times, then he'd look away.

'Let's give him the benefit of the doubt. Maybe he's pretending not to see. I've noticed you don't go out to the warehouses very often.'

She smiled, 'Edith's started going for me, bless her heart. I'm surprised you haven't noticed. It's not difficult to hide a swelling belly behind a typewriter, thank goodness. Mind you, I have to wait to go to the Ladies when he's not around. That's getting harder 'cos I need to pee more often now. I sit with my legs crossed tight.'

'How is the pregnancy going on? I suppose you've seen a doctor now.'

She rubbed her stomach, sat back and stretched out her legs. 'Yes. I got an appointment with one who didn't know me and gave the story that my husband was away. He never blinked an eyelid. I've seen a midwife too. They were all very kind.'

'And you're still settled on adoption?'

She squeezed her eyes tight, 'I'll have to. But the little

one's kicking now and I feel I know him, he's my baby. I talk to him at night, so he'll recognise my voice when he's born. I even sing him lullabies. I hope he can hear me. It's going to kill me when I have to give him up.'

I looked at the clock, 'It's not very late. Do you want to go to Edith's now? I'll come with you, and when we get back we can get you settled for the night. How does that sound?'

E dith and Sidney lived a short bus ride away, but it was a ten-minute walk to the right bus stop. Marion's walk had changed now; she was leaning backwards to balance her growing baby and her footsteps were heavier.

The bus went past some bombed-out houses. A bunch of children had got a fire going in a big tin can, using wood from the damaged building for fuel. Some were warming their hands, but one enterprising lad was toasting bread which he had threaded through a thin bit of metal.

'Got any for me?' one lad shouted.

'Get yer own!' he shouted back.

The kids all needed a good bath and fresh clothes, but they didn't seem a bit bothered. Far from it, they all looked cheerful. A girl, two or three years older, was supervising them.

'Be careful with that wood! Don't get your fingers burnt.'

They took no notice of her.

'Have you noticed more kids around now the bombing's not so bad?' Marion said, 'Ruth's not the only one to want hers back.'

A woman sitting in front of us turned round, 'I got mine back. Missed 'em something rotten I did, for all they're little blighters. I just hope them rotten Nazis don't start the bombing again. We'll stick it out together from now on, come what may.'

'Are your kids at school then?' I asked.

She nodded, 'More or less. Half the school is having lessons in a church hall, and the other half in a pub of all places. When the weather's good, they do some lessons in the pub garden, or even in the churchyard. Spooked some of them out at first, that did, but they've got used to it now. Big classes too.' she looked around, started, and pushed the bell to let the driver know to stop at the next stop, 'I suppose a lot of the teachers are away at war. Nice to meet you two.' She looked at Marion, 'Good luck with your nipper, Love.'

We got off three stops later. Edith and Sidney lived in a terraced house in a road as yet untouched by the bombing, although some roads around it had been less lucky. There were small front gardens, mostly displaying bright flowers. Twice we saw babies sleeping in their prams under the front window.

'Fresh air does them good, doesn't it?' Marion said, sadly, 'I remember my mum saying that.'

Edith and Sidney were weeding their front garden. She was telling him what was weeds and what was flowers. I often didn't know that myself. Bronwyn and I had hardly made a dent in the jungle of our back garden. We'd only cleared enough space to take our chairs outside and sit in the sun when we were lucky enough to be at home at the right time.

Edith noticed us and called hello with a smile, 'This is an unexpected pleasure,' she said. Sidney looked up, a deep frown on his face. He grabbed Edith's arm and stood slightly behind her. To look at him, you'd never think he'd had a head injury, but his full head of hair covered a lot.

'It's nothing to worry about, Sidney,' Edith said, patting his hand, 'it's just two friends from work. You'll like them,' she turned to us, 'why don't you come in. I don't suppose you were just passing, were you?'

'You having a baby?' he said to Marion without even being introduced, 'or are you just fat? It's hard to know.'

Edith squeezed his hand some more, 'She's having a baby, Sidney. Why don't we go in?'

She was wearing an old pair of Sidney's trousers kept up with string, the bottoms turned over several times, and an old cardigan that had seen better days.

'Excuse my gardening clothes,' she said, 'got to save the better stuff with the clothes rationing, haven't we.'

'When's the baby due?' the next-door neighbour said, leaning over the low wall.

'Another few weeks,' Marion said with a forced smile and made her way into Edith's house before she was asked any more questions.

An oval mirror hung over the fireplace in Edith's living room. Two armchairs with wooden arms sat either side of the fireplace, and a sideboard against one wall held a few ornaments.

'Sit down, please,' Edith said, 'Sidney, do you want to stay or carry on gardening?'

For a reply, he simply walked back out the door.

'Can I get you both a cuppa?' she asked.

Marion shook her head, 'It's okay, it's a bit much us coming round without warning like this. It's... well... it's awkward.'

Edith went into the next room, and came back with a wooden dining chair. She sat opposite us, 'What is it then, what's happened?'

'You remember the people I was staying with?' Marion asked.

'That, what was it, Vanessa? She sounded quite a laugh. Has something happened to her?'

'She's only done a runner, hasn't she! Packed up all my stuff while I was at work, and left it there but took everything else. Furniture, everything.'

Edith's jaw dropped open, 'Flipping 'eck! Why on earth would they do that? That's terrible. They didn't even let you know they was going?'

Marion's chin wobbled, and she swallowed back tears. 'No, not a word, and I've been paying my share of the rent to them. I guess they haven't been paying the landlord, and they did a moonlight flit before he caught up with them. The thing is...' she put her hand to her chest.

'What it is,' I said, 'we've been told we can't have a third person staying in our place, so Marion desperately needs accommodation. You said you might be able to put her up.'

She thought for a minute, 'Wait here,' she said and went to the front door. She called Sidney in.

When all four of us were in the living room, she spoke, 'Sidney, this is my friend Marion from work. She looking for somewhere to stay.' She looked at him to make sure he was taking in what she said, 'it's for a few weeks. She'll help pay the rent, which is good. What do you think? Are you happy for her to stay?'

'Will she have the baby here? We want a baby, don't we.' he said in a slow voice.

Edith held his hand, 'It won't be our baby, Sidney, and Marion won't have it here. She'll go away before the baby is born.'

He shrugged his shoulders, 'Okay,' he said, then returned to his weeding.

Marion was looking up at Edith, hope it her eyes.

Edith smiled, 'Looks to me like we're okay. Sidney doesn't say much, but he'd tell me if he didn't like the idea. Can you stay with Lily tonight so I've got time to get things ready? Then you can move in tomorrow. We can talk about money then. Is that okay?'

Marion burst into tears again and hugged Edith hard, thanking her over and over again. Edith hugged her in return then stepped back, 'Are you sure you've got your dates right? You feel a lot further along.'

Marion's chin wobbled again, 'The midwife wasn't sure. She said sometimes you can have a monthly or two, even if you're in the family way. They're just a bit less than usual. I wish I could be sure.'

CHAPTER 21

'Lily, just the girl, glad I caught you!'

I was almost at the gate of the depot, wondering how to spend my evening. My first choice was to go to the British Restaurant and have something to eat, then go to the pictures. I'd never been on my own, but decided it was time to start.

But it wasn't to be.

It was Biggerstaff calling me. My stomach rolled at his voice and I turned round with a false smile on my face.

He put his hand heavily on my shoulder. 'Got a minute?'

I wriggled so that his hand dropped, 'I was about to go home.'

'I've got a little job for you; won't take long.' his shark smile was back, 'I'd like you to deliver this package to a business associate.' He reached into his jacket and took out a small, brown paper package about three inches by four. It was taped closed, and tied with green string.

'What is it?'

He smiled again, 'You don't need to know. It's nothing illegal, just business. And no peeking!' he added with a laugh, 'not that you would, it wouldn't be good for you if you did.'

I rocked slightly on my heels, my mouth dry, 'What do you mean, it wouldn't be good for me?'

He laughed again, 'Nothing, just my little joke. You'll get used to my sense of humour.'

We had to move out of the way as a delivery lorry made its way out of the depot. The driver nodded to us and carried on. A train roared past and two buses passed each other on the road behind us.

He reached into his pocket again and pulled out an envelope. 'The address is in there, it's only Finsbury Park, not far away. And there's enough money for your bus fare and a bit for yourself. Remember, this is just between me and you.'

Without another word he strode off down the street leaving me open mouthed. Mr McDonald had already left for the day so I couldn't tell him in advance what was happening. I remembered that he had said that Biggerstaff would give me something innocent to do first, so I decided to carry on. I'd tell him what had happened next day.

I had no idea how to get to Finsbury Park, so I waited at the bus stop and asked the driver of the first bus that stopped which bus to get. As I walked to the correct bus stop I took off my jacket; although daylight was dimming it was still quite warm.

As I sat on the bus I turned the package over and over, I prodded it and even sniffed at it, but I was no nearer knowing what it contained. It felt like a wad of paper. Then it occurred to me it might be money. That made me shake a bit. I tucked it into an inside pocket, terrified I might lose it. I took the money he'd given me out of the envelope and counted it again. After the cost of the bus fare, what he'd given me wasn't bad; I wouldn't call it generous though. It was enough for the meal and the cinema tickets plus plenty for an ice cream and the bus fare home, and an extra ten shillings I'd put in my savings.

The bus conductress at Finsbury Park gave me directions to the address on Biggerstaff's note. I walked through the streets, noticing they'd had heavy bombing too. They must have been bombed recently because repair squads were still at work doing their best to make houses safe. One was screwing a door back on, another was refitting a widow although much of the glass had gone, a third was shovelling broken bricks and brick dust into the back of a lorry, clouds of dust turning his hair white and making him cough. A woman sat on a pile of bricks, wood and goodness knows what. She looked very relaxed in her works overall, her head in a turban, drinking tea as if she were in her own kitchen. Behind her was an almost intact W.C. laying on its side.

There was a lot of activity on Finsbury Park. Part of it was taken up with army huts being used as barracks. There were anti-aircraft guns on a running track in the middle of the park and barrage balloon units were situated on what had been the football pitch. I stood for a few minutes and watched the soldiers practicing with their guns, remembering my own training days. They seemed so long ago, almost like those days belonged to someone else. Not surprising with all that had happened since. -looked back and thought what my life would have been if I hadn't joined up. I'd probably still be working in the factory, and still be Assistant Manager at the Picture House. Instead I'd made new friends, been to France, learned a new language and had a lot of adventures, some of them terrifying, others fun. As I walked towards the address Biggerstaff had given me I wondered how this adventure would work out. It certainly wouldn't be fun, and I hoped it wouldn't be terrifying.

With street names removed, it was easy to get lost and I had to ask directions three times. Eventually I found the right road which had a row of little shops. Between some of them were doorways leading to flats above. The number I was looking for was one of those, twenty-seven. Taking a deep breath, I knocked on the door and noticed my hand was trembling. A minute later I heard heavy footsteps on the stairs.

'Who is it?' a rough voice shouted.

'I've got a parcel from Mr Biggerstaff,' I called back.

There was the sound of several locks being pulled back and the door opened about six inches. I made out half the face of a fat unshaven man. He put his hand round the door.

'Give it here!' he said.

'I don't know who you are,' I said. I wasn't about to risk giving it to the wrong person.

'I'm Fred Young. Who are you?'

That was the name on the package. He didn't need to know my name. I thrust the package into his hand.

'Is it all there?' he asked.

'No idea, I haven't taken anything.' I turned away not wanting anything more to do with him. The door slammed shut before I'd taken two steps. I couldn't believe he was anyone's idea of a legitimate business contact and I wondered what they were up to.

I looked at the time on a church clock as I walked back to the bus stop. Still time to catch the film if I hurried.

Next morning first thing, I told Mr McDonald what had happened. A frown wrinkled his brow.

'Do you think you were in any danger?' he asked.

'No, I don't think so. The man I gave the package to was a rough 'un, but he wasn't interested in me.'

'Sit down a minute,' he said. 'do you want to carry on with this? You're not in too deep, so you can back out any time.'

I sat back in the chair and inspected my feelings, although it'd been awake half the night thinking about it. 'I'm okay for the time being. Tell you what. Do you have a phone at home?'

He nodded, 'Are you thinking what I'm thinking? If he gives you something to do when I've left like he did yesterday, you can phone me.'

'That's right, as long as I can find a phone box. What do you think?'

He pulled out a piece of paper and scribbled his phone number on it. 'There, call me any time and please, tell me everything that's going on. At the least sign of danger or evidence that he's up to something we'll call in the police.'

But phone boxes in working order can be hard to find.

CHAPTER 22

'Hello Miss,' the boy's voice startled me, and I pulled my eyes from the dogfight taking place high over head. 'I guessed it was you, even though you've got your ARP uniform on,' he said.

I turned, and there in Messenger uniform was Aaron, Ruth's oldest. 'Aren't you too young to be a messenger?' I asked absently.

'I stand in for my mate sometimes - gives me something to do. Don't tell Mum though, will you?'

I raised my eyes to the sky again and saw the two small shapes twisting and turning in the blue sky. Aaron followed my gaze.

'Messerschmitt 110 twin engine,' he announced confidently, 'two crew. And that's a Spitfire that's on to him. Probably a mark five.'

How do lads know this stuff? It's like they're born with it.

Before I answered we heard the faint sound of machine gun fire – a raw sound like the tearing of canvas from the spitfire, to which the German responded with an almost plaintive rat-tat-tat.

Others around the park had stopped to watch the distant struggle. A mother with a pram joined a trio of boiler-suited workmen. Their faces turned heavenward, and hands shielding eyes from the sun, they shared a quiet commentary on the airborne contest.

The glinting of the sun on the shapes seemed to emphasise the energy and desperation of their manoeuvring. The planes moved this way and that through the small fluffy clouds, as if they were in an elaborate dance. But it was a dance to the death. The watchers gasped and cried out when the RAF plane looked in danger, and cheered when it seemed to have the upper hand. The skills both pilots used as they manoeuvred was beyond belief. Then, after another long burst of machine guns, the twin-engined German suddenly broke away. Nose down, he was diving headlong to the north and towards the city. A few people cheered and clapped their hands. 'Well done, mate!' one of the workmen called as if the RAF pilot could hear him.

As sight of the two aircraft was lost the onlookers, still elated by the victory, began to leave. I turned to Aaron and collected my thoughts.

'Now, Aaron, what were you saying about not telling your mother?'

Aaron was about to speak, when he suddenly caught sight of something over my shoulder.

'Miss, they're coming back! They're coming this way!' He pointed urgently at the skyline where, less than half a mile north of the park, the German aircraft seemed to skim the rooftops and chimneys, turning slightly to skirt the park edge. Rather than being distant and somehow unreal as they had been before so high above, they now close to. The grey camouflage and stark black and white crosses fascinated and terrified me. They were almost clear of the park when the

Spitfire fired again, and we clearly saw the brief puffs of smoke that flew behind them, and the firework effects of his bullets as they found their mark on the German. One engine had already stopped on the intruder and the other started to leave a thin trail of black smoke. I held my breath and my stomach turned over with fear as I watched them.

The Messerschmitt turned again, but was too late to stop the RAF plane taking off about two foot of the German's wing, its machine guns turning the section of wing into a shower of debris that trailed the crippled plane. The Spitfire turned again to attack, but before he could inflict more damage the German flew his plane behind the chimneys of the gas works. I was amazed it could still fly, let alone fly so low and fast with part of a wing missing. But the Spitfire followed, and with a burst of machine gun fire that seemed to go on for ever, it ripped through the other wing and the Messersmitt slowed, losing what little height he had.

We watched the fated plane with bated breath until we realised something dreadful.

The plane was coming straight at us and, with both propellers stopped and gliding what seemed like inches above the houses nearest us, it was obvious the pilot had little control.

Aaron and I, along with those close to us, stood rooted to the spot for a moment. People ran in all directions, but I was reluctant to run until I could work out which way was safe.

I almost left it too late.

The plane came closer and I watched it, still spell-bound by the sight. Then Aaron yanked my arm, 'COME ON, MISS!' he shouted, pulling me away. We ran fast, dodging people who were still gaping at the oncoming plane, mouths open, and others who were hurrying to find somewhere safe. On one side was a railway line with a wire fence so it was impossible to go that way. We ran the other way, across the road and into a playground. A small brick building with a flat roof was in the corner; a public toilet. Hoping that the plane sliding out of control wouldn't kill us, we dived into it. It smelled awful.

We heard the distinctive roar of the Spitfire as it passed low over the park, but then all was ominously quiet. I wondered if the German had recovered, and taken again to the chase. Or perhaps he'd stretched his glide and was now well clear of us and the park. I was about to take a cautious look outside when there was a massive crash and the ground shook as the plane finally hit the ground. This was closely followed by a series of bangs and crashes as it hit trees, lamps posts and the fence beside the railway line.

We looked at each other, and Aaron grinned, 'Come on, let's see what's happened,' he said. He saw it as an adventure, but I was shaking with relief at being alive.

What a sight met our eyes. The plane had come to a stop on the railway line, tearing down the wire fence and blocking the track completely. We were the first to reach the wreck, and saw the cockpit was concertinaed like a piece of screwed up paper. As we watched, one of the forward-facing guns dropped off with a thud. The propellers were bent back and twisted, with some blades snapped off. They'd been flung some distance from the plane. It was amazing they hadn't cut anyone in half.

Dust was still rising from the trail the plane had carved across the park. I pulled my hanky out of my bag and put it over my mouth and nose, indicating to Aaron that he should do the same.

'Bloody 'ell,' someone who had approached us from my right said, 'I wonder if it's going to catch fire?'

'Never mind that,' someone else said, 'do you think there's anyone inside still alive?'

'No one could have survived in the cockpit,' said another with some confidence.

They were right, but behind the cockpit the body of the plane was relatively intact, and I knew from my ARP work that people can sometimes survive beyond all expectations.

'Oh, my God,' someone nearby shouted, 'What if a train's coming? It'll smash straight into this lot!'

I turned to Aaron, 'I'm going to find a phone box to tell the emergency services. You stay well back.'

I knew the area and ran to the next street. People were in the road, wondering if a bomb had gone off.

'Do we need to go to the shelter?' someone asked.

'No, it's a plane down on the railway line. Stay well away.'

I realised everyone needed to know, so I cupped my hands and shouted, 'STAY AWAY FROM THE RAILWAY LINE! DANGER! THERE MAY BE AN EXPLOSION!'

I shouted it several times, and a few people turned back but some carried on. My ARP experience had taught me that with some people curiosity overcomes their sense of fear.

It would take ages to clear the fallen plane, so I needed to get a message down the line to stop all trains.

Luckily the phone box was working, and I quickly passed on the message, then ran back to the crash site. To my horror, Aaron and a man were climbing on to the plane. It rocked, creaked and groaned under their weight and I was terrified it might explode at any minute. The crowd hadn't thinned, and some people were shouting encouragement, while others looked on wide-eyed with fear.

'What are you doing?' I shouted, 'it's dangerous!'

Aaron heard me, 'Getting the gunner out. We think he's

177

still alive.'

The man he was with reached into the shattered rear cockpit. The machine gun still stuck out of it.

'Hold my legs!' he called to Aaron, then using his elbow promptly began smashing what remained of the cockpit glass. Each move made the plane wobble alarmingly. All the time he was shouting to the gunner, 'Don't worry! We'll get you!'

'Don't suppose he'll understand a word of that!' someone near me muttered.

Aaron held the man's legs to keep what was left of the plane in balance and then very slowly, the man reached into the cockpit. For a minute or two his whole upper body vanished as his head went well into the space. He was grunting from the effort of whatever he was doing.

'He'll be getting him out of his safety harness,' the man behind me said, 'bloody dangerous. He needs a medal.'

Painfully slowly, the man backed out, still with Aaron holding his legs. They both slid down the plane a little as the top of the gunner's head appeared. He was wearing a leather helmet, but his head was down and his face was hidden. The man wriggled back up, shouting 'Hold on to me!' The words made the gunner looked up. He looked so young. Even with blood on his face and a look of terror in his eyes, it was obvious he was only about seventeen. Without moving his head his eyes moved from left to right as if looking for an escape route. But soon the rescuer made him understand, and he put his arms round the man's neck. There was sudden movement, and we saw all of him.

'He'll be standing on his seat,' the man near me said, 'let's hope he's got enough strength to get out.'

Painfully slowly, he was pulled out, his uniform ripping with every move.

That was when we saw and heard it.

A train coming down the track.

'HURRY!' several people in the crowd shouted, 'TRAIN COMING!'

Our heads turned again and again from the drama on the plane to the approaching train as if we were watching a tennis match.

The gunner had a cut on his cheek that was dripping blood down his face and neck and onto his uniform jacket. Aaron was almost on the ground, and I held his arm to help him down, not that he needed me. But I needed to feel useful.

The train was getting nearer and louder, and people scattered. I yanked Aaron, and we ran across the road again, but stopped to see what happened.

The rescuer pulled the gunner away from the plane and railway lines and laid him down on the ground. The lad tried to get up, but he was weak and the effort was too much; each time he tried he collapsed back down again.

There was a tremendous screeching of brakes and the train's hooter tooted again and again. Then, less than twenty yards from the plane, it squealed to a halt. The carriages rocked on their wheels and I held my breath expecting them to topple over, but to my surprise they righted themselves.

Sirens announced the arrival of an ambulance and two police cars. The ambulance people ran over to the train, and the police to the gunner.

The gunner was laying on the ground, his rescuer watching over him. A small crowd were watching too, some sympathetic because of his age and some wanting him strung up immediately. His eyes were wide with terror, and he kept looking from one of us to another. His look alternated between pleading and fear.

'Tote mich nicht, tone mich nicht,' he said over and over again, and tried to put his hands up in surrender. But one arm was broken and each time he tried to lift it he whimpered with pain. Even so, it was easy to understand his meaning.

The police handcuffed him, and the movement made him yell with pain again.

'He needs an ambulance,' I told the nearest officer.

'Yes, and he'll get one when some more arrive. First we want to help the people off the train. They're not the bloody enemy trying to kill us.'

'Anyone speak German?' I shouted. At first no one answered. It wasn't something people wanted to own up to. Then, to my surprise, Aaron spoke up, 'I can speak it a little bit.'

'Can you tell him we're not going to kill him. We'll take him to a hospital, and then the police station.'

In a hesitant voice, correcting himself several times, he passed on my message. The gunner looked from him to me to the police. His expression went from hope to disbelief and back again. I'd read that Nazi propaganda lied that we were all monsters, and he must have been wondering if we were genuine.

He was well looked after, so I told Aaron to follow me to the train. Two more ambulances had arrived, so the crews were helping people off the trains and triaging the injured. Through the window I saw Bronwyn walking the length of the train, looking for anyone too injured to get themselves out. A minute later she stuck her head out of the door,

'OVER HERE!' she shouted.

An ambulance man went to help her, and I took over his job. Most people had bumps and cuts from being thrown forward, and a few had more serious injuries from flying luggage. As we worked, two more ambulances arrived, and we soon had a system going. The walking injured were sent to a nearby rest centre, guided by Aaron and another ARP warden. Those needing medical treatment were taken to hospital by ambulance. Luckily, the train wasn't full, otherwise the disaster would have been a lot more serious.

The clean-up crew were already at work doing their best to clear the plane off the track. When they uncovered the pilot's body the general hubbub stopped and several people crossed themselves. Others said things like 'Bloody good job, Jerry Scum.' and a few spat in his direction. His body was quickly driven away.

Aaron came back and worked alongside me for another hour, then there was nothing further for us to do. The clean-up squads would be there all night, but we decided to go back to Aaron's house. He wasn't too sure about that.

'You won't tell Mum about the messenger job, will you? You promised.'

'Where are your normal clothes?'

'In my saddlebag.'

'Nip over to that toilet and get changed, then we'll head to your place.'

I didn't want to lie to Ruth, so I left that to Aaron. He said he'd bumped into me when he'd been on his way home, and together we'd seen the plane crash. It was a very edited version of the truth. I suppose I lied by omission, but he was a good lad, and I didn't want to get him in trouble.

When Ruth heard he'd helped rescue the gunner she went white, red, then white again.

'YOU DID WHAT!' she shouted. 'YOU SILLY BOY! You might have died saving someone who would have killed you in an instant just because you're a Jew.'

He looked down at his scuffed shoes, 'But he wasn't

much older than me, Mum. And he was really scared! You'd have felt sorry for him if you'd seen him.'

'He wasn't as scared as all those people who have been murdered by his countrymen.'

I interrupted, 'One way to look at it is that Aaron showed himself to be a better person than any of those Germans. You can be very proud of him.'

'But the danger! The German might have had a gun and shot him! The plane could have exploded or collapsed on him!' she covered her face with her hands, 'I can't stand thinking about it.'

Aaron stood shifting from one foot to the other uncomfortably.

'The good thing is,' I said, trying to keep my voice calm, 'none of that happened. He's here, and he's safe. If he'd been an RAF gunner and shot down, you'd have liked to think some kind person would help him.'

'Those Nazis wouldn't!' she said, her jaw jutting and eyes blazing.

'But the resistance fighters would,' Aaron said, 'I've been reading all about them. They're the ones who are really brave. They help loads of English people escape. Jews too. And not all Germans agree with what Hitler is doing. They don't!'

He was just about as tall as his mother, and went over and put his head on her shoulder, 'Don't be cross, Mum. I'm okay, we're all okay.'

After a brief pause her shoulders relaxed, and she patted the top of his head, 'Silly boy! Go and make yourself a sandwich then off to bed with you. Your sisters are already there.'

When he'd left the room she turned to me. 'Do you have to go back on duty or can you stay for a while?'

I sat, or rather fell, into one of her armchairs. 'I've signed off for the night, so my time's my own.'

She touched my shoulder, 'I'm grateful you were there to keep an eye on the silly boy!'

Then she headed for the kitchen. I took off my shoes and rubbed my aching feet. I leaned back in the armchair and drifted off for a few minutes, then woke with a start when she came back into the room carrying a loaded tray. The cups and saucers rattled against the tea spoons, and I was pleased to see a plate of biscuits on the tray, too.

We heard Aaron getting ready for bed. 'Night, Mum,' he called, 'love you!'

'Love you too, you silly boy,' she shouted back.

We drank two cups of what passed for coffee and demolished the biscuits, then she got a bottle of wine and two glasses out of her sideboard. It seemed very sophisticated to me; I'd hardly ever drunk wine, and didn't know anyone who kept some at home.

'I allow myself one bottle of wine to last over the week,' Ruth said, struggling with the bottle opener, 'but this seems like a special occasion so I'd be honoured if you'd join me.'

She poured two small glasses, and we toasted our good health. For maybe twenty minutes we talked about trivial things at work, then, 'Can I tell you a secret?' she asked.

By now we were on our second glass of wine. I wondered what it was about me that made people want to tell me their secrets.

'Of course you can,' I said, 'I'm good at keeping secrets.'

She put down her wine glass, sat back in her chair and wrung her hands. 'Well, it's… it's… sort of difficult. Embarrassing.'

I put my glass down, too. 'Take your time, there's no hurry. And if you change your mind, you don't need to tell me a thing.'

She got up and closed the living room door, 'I don't want the children to hear this because they don't know.'

Don't know what? I itched to ask.

She went into the kitchen and came back with a glass of water. Then she sat cradling it in both hands.

'I'm afraid I've been lying to you all this time. All of you at the office,' she looked down, avoiding my eyes.

'Lying? That doesn't sound at all like you.'

She looked over to the sideboard, 'Do you remember the first time you came round here you commented that Rubin's photo wasn't out with the others?'

I nodded, wondering where this was going.

'Well, it's about him and me. We've been married fifteen years, you know. Our families introduced us and encouraged us to get together. They both thought it was a good match, and that was very important for them and their standing in the community.'

I frowned, unsure what to say, 'That's a long time. Was it a good match? Were they right?'

Her shoulders slumped, 'It was, or at least I thought it was. We had a lot in common: our religion, our family, our friends, even our outlook on life. We had our three wonderful children, and did most things together. One night a week he went out with his friend from work, but otherwise he was an ideal husband. Well, a bit lazy about the house but most men are, aren't they.'

I picked up my wine glass again and took another sip. The wind was getting up, and I heard it rustling trees in her garden. 'What happened?' I asked when she'd been silent for a while.

'I've told you all he's working in Scotland. That's true, but it's a longer story than that. The truth is, he's left me.'

I leaned over and put my hand on her arm, 'Oh, Ruth, I'm

so sorry, that must be awful when you have the little ones.'

She bit her lip, 'It is. It's hard for anyone, but especially someone with my upbringing. That's why I moved me and the children to somewhere new. My parents, they're elderly and very stuck in their ways and well, they don't understand why he doesn't come back to me. They think it's a fling with a younger woman, and he'll get over it. They're the only ones I've told because they kept asking awkward questions.'

'Gosh, that must have been a hard conversation.'

'It was. I can't tell you how difficult. They're ashamed of me, of course. I can't keep a man, that's what they think. It's all my fault. They've told me that many times.'

I picked up the wine bottle and filled our glasses, 'It's not up to me to say, Ruth, but they seem very unkind. They should have been supporting you.'

She wrung her hands again, 'They think I... well... I didn't keep him happy in the... you know... bedroom. But they didn't know the whole story. Oh dear, I shouldn't be talking to you about this, you a single girl and everything.'

'I think what goes on between a husband and wife in the bedroom is no business of anyone but them.'

She got up and adjusted the black out curtains that were already fine. 'In a way they were right,' she said with her back to me. She moved over to the sideboard and moved the photos of the children half an inch, 'he left me for someone younger, you know. That sounds like a familiar story, doesn't it? The woman who's stood by his side for years gets thrown aside for a newer model.'

She plonked herself down in her chair again and took a long glug of wine.

My heart went out to her. Poor Ruth, deserted like so many other women have been. 'That's awful Ruth, and such a familiar story.'

She got up again and this time, she went and put the kettle on, then turned it off again. 'It's not the old story though,' she said when she came back in empty handed.

She sat down again, 'He's... he's...' she put her head in her hands and burst into tears, great sobs moving her shoulders up and down.

I went over, sat on the arm of her chair, and put my arm round her shoulders without saying anything.

It took her a minute or two to get herself back under control. She wiped her cheeks and blew her nose. 'I'm going to say it quickly. Yes, I am. He's left me for a younger man! A man! I'm so ashamed!'

I could have fallen off the chair. Another man! I'd never heard of a married man going with another man. I couldn't understand how that happened at all. If they liked men, why did they marry women? It was beyond my understanding. But looking as shocked and confused as I felt wouldn't help Ruth. I went and knelt in front of her, taking her hands. 'But why are you ashamed? You didn't do anything.'

She squeezed my hands in return, 'What if it's my fault? What if I wasn't a proper wife like he wanted? He was never one to make a lot of... you know... demands. I thought that was just how he was. When the children were little and I was always tired, it was a bit of a relief to be honest.'

I went back to my seat but leaned towards her. 'I don't know about these things Ruth, but there is no good blaming yourself. It was his choice, not yours. You didn't push him away. He decided to go. Perhaps it's time to let go of guilt, and make a life for yourself. What do your children say?'

She sighed heavily, 'I haven't told them. They think their father is just working away. He writes to them every week or two, and we have an agreement that he won't say what's happened.'

'But what about when the war ends, and he doesn't have to be in Scotland?'

She shook her head, 'I suppose we'll say he has a job up there or something. He can come to visit the children sometimes, but I've insisted they never meet the man he's with. It would simply be too much for them. And me.'

She turned and grasped my hands in hers, 'Promise me on your mother's life you won't tell a soul. What he's doing is against the law and he could go to prison. Think of my poor children!'

Before she said more we heard crying from upstairs. She stood up, 'It will be Judith, she still has nightmares sometimes about that awful farm woman. I'll settle her. Make yourself another drink if you like.'

Ten minutes later she came downstairs looking calmer. She had washed her face and brushed her hair. 'Judith has gone back to sleep now. Thank you for listening to me, Lily. I'm sorry if I've weighed you down with my problems, but it was such a relief to tell someone.'

I picked up the glass of water I got while she was upstairs. 'Actually, there's something I'd like to talk to you about if you don't mind.'

'Of course, of course. Anything. Nothing you say will be more shocking than my news.' I was glad to see she raised a brief smile.

I hesitated, wondering how to explain, 'It's like this. You know I've been engaged to Edward for ages...'

'And you had a row a little while ago. Have you made that up yet?'

I shook my head, 'He has written to me and apologised, but I haven't replied yet. The thing is, well, that row made me face up to a few things.'

'What sort of things?'

I paused, wondering how to explain what had happened, 'When we got engaged I was a different person to the one I am now. I was much more timid, didn't know my way round the world. Since I joined the ATS and ARP I've had so many adventures, I've lived in Paris, got new friends and done all sorts of things. The problem is, I've changed and now I realise my feelings have as well.'

She clasped her hands together, 'Are you trying to say you don't love him any more?'

I took a deep breath, 'I suppose I am. We've seen each other so rarely since we met that the truth is we hardly know each other. There's nothing wrong with him, I'm not blaming him. We've just grown apart.' I felt dreadful saying these words; my stomach knotted with stress even thinking about them.

'It sounds as if you've been in love with a memory for a long time, not the real man.'

I looked up, 'That's exactly right. And our letters have got less frequent too, and when I think about it, they're not as loving as they used to be. More as if we're just writing to a friend, not someone you're in love with.'

She stood up and buttoned her cardigan, then sat down again. 'Are you sure it's not just that you're angry because of the argument you had?'

'I've thought and thought about that. I was angry. I couldn't believe he would think I'd behaved that way. He should know me better. But then I got thinking. It might have been because we don't really know each other any more.'

I remembered the wonderful days when we first met.

Those days just before this awful war started that seemed like a dream now. Our meeting when someone tried to rob me at The Picture House; those picnics and dances; his kindness and support. He was a good man - there was no way I could think otherwise. He still was a good man, despite our argument. This falling out of love wasn't his fault, but it wasn't mine either. It wasn't something I'd chosen to do. Perhaps it started when he was missing in action, presumed dead. Over that long time I'd adjusted to life without him. I'd mourned, although I hadn't been sure he was really dead, but I had been forced by work, the ARP volunteering and the war to get on with my life. I felt like a widow recovering from her loss.

'Are you okay?' Ruth asked, 'you look miles away.'

I shook myself out of my daydream. 'I'm fine, just remembering good times.'

'Are you sure this is how you feel?' she asked, 'it would be a mistake to break off your engagement if you're not sure.'

I searched my feelings, like prodding a painful tooth, 'Yes, I'm sure. To be honest, there have been whole days when I haven't thought about him at all. We've spent so little time together. If the war hadn't got in the way and it was a normal courtship, we probably wouldn't have got engaged until much later.'

'Mmm, so many wartime relationships have been speeded up. My mother used to talk about her friends' romances in the Great War. Several got engaged or married before their men went off to fight. A lot of the men never came back, of course.' she shook herself, 'anyway, enough of my chattering. If you're certain, what will you do about it?'

'I'll have to go to see him. I don't think it's something that can be dealt with by letter.'

CHAPTER 23

I wrote to Edward asking to meet him. The letter took hours and many attempts to write. In truth, it was a *Dear John* letter, although not explicitly so as it was asking to meet. I wanted to give him a hint of what was to come, yet not hurt his feelings. He didn't deserve to be hurt, even though he had misunderstood me about my visit to Colchester.

With his army commitments and mine, the date took some sorting out. I hoped to meet somewhere neutral in London that was convenient for him. He suggested The Cafe Royal, which was much more expensive than my usual eating places. I don't know why, but I hadn't told Bronwyn or anyone other than Ruth what I was planning. Maybe I thought I'd change my mind once I saw Edward again.

We'd agreed to meet at the restaurant at twelve thirty, and I was five minutes late on purpose. I knew I'd feel silly sitting there on my own waiting for him. My self-confidence was a lot better than it used to be, but I still didn't feel good enough for somewhere like The Cafe Royal. I stood outside for a minute, summoning up the courage to go in. Then I rehearsed again what I was going to say, took a deep breath, and pushed open the door.

The maitre'd, looked me up and down, 'Can I help you, Miss?' he asked. I was glad to be wearing uniform - he'd probably have looked down his nose at my civvies clothes.

'I'm here to meet Edward Halpern.'

He consulted a book on the little table in front of him, running his finger down the lines until he found Edward's name.

'Come this way, Miss,' he said and walked ahead, his footsteps muted by the thick cream carpet.

Even though it was daylight, the room sparkled with lights reflecting off the mirrors on every wall. Each table had a starched white tablecloth, a small vase of flowers and immaculate sparkling glasses and cutlery. At one table a chef in his white jacket and tall hat was carving a big joint of beef. A waiter in a dinner suit and bow tie served vegetables to a couple nearby. The woman at the table had a red hat on with a tall feather that threatened to poke the waiter in the eye. There was a gentle hubbub of voices, and the smell of food and expensive perfume. Those women who weren't in uniform were elegant and sophisticated.

Edward was studying the menu as I approached him, and I was almost beside him when he looked up. Like me, he was in uniform, and he looked as handsome as ever. My heart gave a little jolt when he smiled, but I was aware it was a different feeling from those I'd had before. This time it was nervousness.

'Lily!' he cried, and held his hands out. I held both of them, and he kissed me on the cheek, smelling of his familiar cologne. 'It's so good to see you,' he said with a broad smile.

I took off my cap and had barely sat beside him before a waiter thrust a menu in my hand. There was already a bottle of wine on the table, and the waiter poured us both glasses.

'I've already had a look at the menu,' he said, 'why don't you choose, then the waiters will give us some peace to talk.'

No egg on toast in The Cafe Royal. There was a notice on the top of the menu I'd never seen before:

*'By order of the Ministry of Food no more than three courses may be served at a meal, nor may any person have more than one main course marked * and one subsidiary dish marked ◎ or alternatively two side dishes marked ***

Lucky people to have three courses, I thought, but I'd never manage to eat that much even if I could afford it.

I took ages choosing, delaying the moment when I would have to say what I'd come to say. In the end, I chose Game Pie because I'd never tried it before, and it cost an amazing five shillings. I guessed Edward would pay the bill. If I had to pay my share I'd be living on bread and dripping for a week. Five shillings would buy me several meals at The British Restaurant.

When the waiter had taken my order, Edward turned to me and reached for my hand. 'It's lovely to see you, Lily. How are things with you?'

My mouth went dry. I wasn't certain I could make small talk when there was something so important I needed to say, but I had to try.

'I'm fine, nothing much has changed. How is your work?'

He gave a little smile, 'It's okay, but you know I can't talk about it. But, Lily, you asked to see me so I know it's something important. I want to apologise again for misjudging you last time we met. You were right to be angry with me. I shouldn't have believed what my friend said, I should have known you better.'

My heart rate sped up and my hands became clammy. 'It's sort of about that,' I said, and my voice sounded as if it belonged to someone else, 'the misunderstanding set me thinking about our relationship. You believing your friend made me realise how little we know each other now. We've hardly spent any time together since we got engaged. With being apart and not able to talk about our work we have much less connection than we used to have.'

He didn't say anything, just looked at me and listened.

'So, well, I'm not sure how to say this Edward but... I'm a different person after all this time and the experiences I've had. It's nothing to do with you. But...'

He squeezed my hand, 'Go on, Lily, just say what you want to say.'

It was hard to breathe, 'I'm so sorry but I don't think I love you any more,' my words tumbled over each other. 'It's not you, and I haven't found anyone else, it's just I've changed so much and things are different and...'

'And you don't love me any more,' he sounded sad rather than angry.

I nodded and wiped a tear from my cheek. 'I'm so sorry. You're the best of men, really the best - honest and true. I'll never find anyone as wonderful as you, but those intense feelings have drifted away. I truly wish they hadn't, but I can't live a lie. It's not fair on either of us.'

He let go of my hand and sat back, his face unreadable. 'So this is the end?'

I covered a little sob with my hanky, 'I hope it's not, Edward. I hope we can always be friends.'

The waiter came with his starter. He looked at us and must have seen something serious was happening, because he poured more wine and moved away very quickly. Edward picked up his knife and fork, put them down again, and sighed heavily.

'I don't know what to say, Lily. I didn't expect this, but to tell you the truth, I've been feeling the same. I hope that won't upset you.'

I blinked hard, unable to believe I'd heard right.

He cut into his asparagus and took a bite without looking at me.

'You feel the same?' I said with a lighter heart, 'really? You're not just saying this to make me feel better?'

He ate some asparagus. 'In fact, I'd been trying to pluck up courage to talk to you about it. Are you sure you won't try this asparagus? It's delicious.'

He held a piece on his fork for me to taste. A moment earlier I couldn't have eaten a thing, but I leaned forward and took it from his fork. I'd never had it before. I liked it, but wondered why people made such a fuss about it.

He ate more then put his knife and fork together and caught the waiter's eye to let him know he could take the plate away.

'You've probably noticed my letters have been a bit, well, different for a while.'

I nodded. 'I have, more like a letter to a friend. Mine have been the same as well.'

He took a sip of his wine and I did the same. 'I've found it very hard to write to you for ages, trying to get the right words without being dishonest. Things have changed for me too.'

His shoulders tensed and his cheeks reddened. It took a few seconds for the penny to drop.

'Have you found someone else, Edward?'

He fiddled with the cutlery. 'Sort of. I want to be straight with you. There's someone at work I'm attracted to. I haven't done anything about it. Nothing at all. But we seem to find excuses to spend time together. I didn't want to ask her out while the situation between us was so unclear.'

'But I'd ended our engagement. I gave you back your ring.'

'I wasn't sure if you meant it. You were in a temper, and rightly so. You didn't reply to my letter apologising, but I couldn't take that to mean we were definitely finished without speaking to you. Not after all we've been to each other in the past.'

I felt as if a weight had been lifted from my shoulders. This was the last response I expected from him, but the best possible one. I tested my feelings to see if I was jealous about him finding someone else, but I only felt happiness for him. He deserved to be with someone who cared for him.

'I hope she's someone your mother would approve of!' I said with a wicked grin. She'd never thought I was up to scratch.

He smiled too, 'Frankly, I don't care. It's not about her, is it?'

We spent the rest of the meal talking over all times like friends who hadn't seen each other for years. We were so comfortable together once that initial conversation was over, and I began to believe we would be friends in the future.

'What about you, Lily?' he asked after a while, 'have you found anyone else?'

'No, there's nobody, and I'm not looking to be honest. I don't have time anyway between work and the ARP duties. Maybe one day. Who knows?'

He raised his glass, 'Here's to our future, separate but friends for ever.'

I told Bronwyn the news that night. Her jaw dropped open. 'You've broken off with him? How long have you been thinking about that? You dark horse!'

It was a pleasant late afternoon as I left the Depot, heading for the bus stop to take me to the ARP station for my evening duty. I stopped and stretched after a long day bent over a typewriter, noticing how the low sun threw long shadows from the warehouse units, and reflected on the barrage balloons floating overhead.

I was almost at the bus stop when Biggerstaff stepped out of a side street and tapped me on the shoulder. He hadn't asked me to do anything since the package delivery, and I hoped he'd forgotten all about me. No such luck.

'Lovely to see you, Lily,' he said with his sinister smile, 'Can we have a quick word?'

'I don't have long,' I said, 'I'm on ARP duty this evening.'

'Quite the goodie goodie, aren't you!' he said with a smirk, 'this won't take a minute, I'm off to a meeting myself. I just wanted to ask if you'd seen anything unusual in my dockets.'

I recalled my suspicions about the number of returns. Should I mention it?

'We've had a few returns, but that's to be expected,' I said.

His face relaxed, 'That's good to hear. I like to keep my customers happy. Will you tell me if there's anything amiss?'

I nodded.

'There's a good girl. I'll make it up to you next time we see each other.'

He glanced at his watch, 'Is that the time? I must be off. Goodbye for now and remember, keep mum!' he mimed zipping his mouth.

He set off at a pace over the level crossing and towards the shopping street. I don't know what came over me, but I decided to follow him. I'd probably been reading too many detective novels.

It was difficult to keep up with him, because he had much longer legs than me. Once or twice I had to do a short run. All the films I'd seen where someone was being tailed involved the follower diving into shop doorways or ducking behind cars at regular intervals. I expected to do the same, but didn't need to. He walked briskly, not looking left or right. My adrenaline was high, even though I'd thought of a good excuse if he saw me. I'd say I'd remembered something I needed to tell him. I hadn't got as far as thinking what that was; it would have to be a spur-of-the-moment decision.

Then he stopped without warning, and got a piece of paper out of his pocket.

A family with two children and a big pram were near me and I hid behind them, peeking round to see what he would do next. One of the children thought I was playing a game with her and waved at me, giggling. I smiled and waved back. Luckily the family walked slowly, so I wasn't in danger of catching up with him.

He studied the paper for a minute, gave a little nod and

continued on his way, taking the next left turn. I'd never seen on detective films how you followed someone round a corner without being spotted. It wasn't a road I knew, and I worried it might be very quiet with no shops or anything to hide behind.

I wasn't far wrong. It was a residential street with a mixture of houses and scattered small businesses like a garage, a bike shop and a bakers'. Luckily for me, Biggerstaff didn't stop again; he knocked on a door a few houses along from the bakers' shop and was quickly let in. I hid behind a small queue at the shop watching the house. It had biggish windows and a front garden. There was an alleyway at the side.

This street was unfamiliar to me. What was I to do? If I went back to Mr McDonald and said I'd followed Biggerstaff to this address he'd say Biggerstaff was probably visiting his mother or something. But soon another two men went into the house. It might have been a family gathering, but it seemed increasingly unlikely. I stood and frowned, trying to decide what to do. The first option was safe; the second might be dangerous.

I recalled my days retreating from Paris with Bronwyn and two other ATS girls. We'd faced much worse danger than peeking in someone's window. I gave myself a mental kick up the bottom and decided that if no-one else came within five minutes, I'd go and try to see in the window.

That five minutes went slower than a man running with a piano on his back. I pretended to be waiting to go in the bakers'. Not surprisingly, the women queuing for bread kept giving me funny looks when I let them go ahead of me.

After five minutes, I walked towards the house with a confident step. Appearing nervous would be a certain give-away if Biggerstaff spotted me. The house was similar to others in the row. The small front garden had some paving slabs and a small selection of well-tended flowers. The front door, no different from its neighbours, was dark blue and scratched around the keyhole. I went past briskly and took a quick look at the window, but my luck was out. There were net curtains and the usual safety crosses, so I couldn't see a thing. Continuing to walk, but much slower, I pondered what to do next. Then I noticed a smaller road leading left.

The road led to a park. A children's play park with trees swaying in the breeze and birds chirping happily. A cat sat in a patch of sun cleaning itself, ignoring everything around it. There was a swing, a slide, a roundabout and a few benches. A mother pushed her daughter on a swing while trying to keep hold of a toddler who wanted to escape. Two bigger lads took it in turns on the slide, going feet first, then head first, chortling with laughter. A little further away a bunch of teenagers sat in a circle smoking cigarettes. Whatever they talked about caused a lot of laughs.

I turned back towards the rear of the houses. They were separated from the park by dilapidated wooden fences and gates. While I stood there a woman went into a houses a few doors from the one I'd worked out was the one to watch. Seeing her gave me an idea.

Did I dare try the gate? I sucked my teeth thinking of an excuse if caught, then it came to me. Wrong house. Simple as that. 'You mean Julie doesn't live here? Sorry!'

That's what I'd say.

The gate was made of wooden planks, all past their best. One was leaning over making an elongated triangle without wood, so it was easy to see into the garden through the crack. The garden was empty. As quietly as possible, I tried the latch. Its squeak was enough to wake the dead, or so it seemed. But no-one in the play ground noticed. To my surprise, the gate opened first time. I pushed it very slowly, ready to make a run for it if challenged. That was stupid, allowing the alibi I'd invented.

Walking softly in army shoes isn't easy, but the path was half covered in grass from the overgrown lawn and that muffled my footsteps. I had to watch where I trod, and narrowly missed stepping into some cat do-do.

I had no intention of going into the house, just to peek through the window. Like the front, it had criss-cross tapes, but this time no net curtains. My heart thumped so loudly it was amazing no-one in the house heard it. I tip-toed across the back of the house to one corner of the window. Inside, several men stood around with bottles of beer in their hands. They seemed very relaxed and friendly. Two men were pinning a flag on the wall to my right. At first I couldn't see what it was, and expected it to be the flag of one country. But as they smoothed the fabric I recognised it and my body went cold.

It was the flag of the Blackshirts; the fascist union that had been banned some time before. Rectangular, the back-ground was red with a white circle in the middle. Within the middle was a white thunder flash with a dark blue surround. I didn't know a lot about Blackshirts, but I knew they were pro-Nazi and anti-Jewish. They'd been banned because of the violence they'd used at their rallies. The organisation's aim was to undermine the government.

I kept my head down, although it meant I only saw a part of the room. That was five or six men. When the men at the front had the flag to their liking, one of them clapped his hands to get attention. Then I saw they all wore arm-bands with the Blackshirts logo. There was no mistake.

I heard the scraping of chairs as the men moved to take their seats. Then, as he was about to sit down, I saw Biggerstaff who still had a bottle of beer in his hand. He was chatting to another man, and they clinked their bottles together and laughed at something. The leader clapped his hands again and Biggerstaff turned.

That's when it happened.

He saw me.

CHAPTER 25

*I*mmobilised for a second, my mind flashed back to all I knew about him. The photo in the old newspaper where he was with a parade of Blackshirts. The higher than usual number of returns of guns and boots. Him wanting me to be his spy.

This was his way of sabotaging the British war effort. Who knew how many other tricks he was up to.

He was a traitor.

*H*e recognised me and his eyes opened wide for a second, then narrowed. He said something I couldn't hear and pointed straight at me. The men around him turned towards the window, and glared at me, cold eyed.

I turned and ran out of the garden as if my life depended on it. Perhaps it did. I couldn't go back to the road, they'd come out of the front door, and catch up with me in no time. I had to go through the park.

I quickly looked at the layout and ran towards an exit, heart pounding. As I ran past the family the toddler finally made an escape, and I almost ran into her.

The pause cost me precious seconds.

'YOU! STOP!' a harsh voice behind me shouted.

I looked at the teenage boys who were watching all this with interest. 'Quick, save me!' I shouted, 'Help!'

They obviously thought it was a good game. Two of them leapt up and ran towards me.

For an awful moment, I thought they were going to catch me and hand me over to the Blackshirts. But I was wrong. They swerved behind me. Running at top speed, I didn't catch what they did but I heard a thud, then terrible swearing. I glanced over my shoulder, and the two lads and the older man were in a heap on the grass.

'Run, Miss! We've got him,' one of the lads shouted. I smiled and gave them a thumbs up and carried on running. The exit seemed a mile away, and all the time I worried others may be coming after me. My breathing grew ragged and I got a stitch in my side.

Then I was out on the road and relieved there were people about. I could hide among them, and whoever it was would be less likely to grab me in public. It couldn't be Biggerstaff; he didn't look that fit. I dodged into a grocery shop and bent over with my palms on my knees, trying to get my breath back.

'You okay, Miss?' an assistant said in a concerned voice, 'do you need help?'

I stood more upright, trying to get air into my lungs, 'I'm okay, thanks,' I said, 'just give me a while.' I went to the window, stood back, and looked both ways. There was no sign of any men looking around as if searching for someone.

'Do you mind if I wait here a minute? I'm trying to avoid someone.'

A customer came in, and the assistant turned to serve her. He smiled at me, letting me know I could stay. I peered at every man who walked past, not that I knew what any of them looked like. I did my best to see who was in passing cars, but reflections stopped me from seeing in properly.

My breathing gradually slowed to normal and I wiped the sweat from my face.

Then it hit me.

I may have got away for now, but Biggerstaff had seen me. He wasn't going to let me be free to spoil all his plans.

He would want me dead.

~

'Where's the nearest police station?' I asked the assistant.

He continued putting the lady's shopping in her bag and they both turned to look at me.

'The cop shop?' he asked, 'I can't say I'm sure. Is it something I can help with?'

But the lady interrupted him. 'There's one further up the street, on the corner of Wilberforce Road. Opposite the bombed out church. You can't miss it. Go left outside the shop here.'

With tentative steps, I went to the shop doorway and looked around. It looked safe. Not wanting to draw attention to myself, I strode along the pavement, but I looked everywhere for danger.

I spotted the blue police station sign and smiled. Almost there.

Then a car, a Hillman Super Snipe, slowed down and kept

pace with me. Another car beeped its horn angrily and over-took the Hillman, the driver making a rude gesture.

The Hillman's window wound down. At first I didn't grasp the significance, then realisation dawned and I was too scared to turn my head to see who was driving. Instead I walked faster and faster.

'GET IN!' the words pierced like a wolf's howl.

It was Biggerstaff.

'Get in!' he shouted again.

I held back a scream and ran for the police station, arms pumping.

His car kept pace with me again. 'You stupid girl!' he shouted, 'get in!'

I slammed open the police station doors and ran to the desk. I leaned on it with my elbows, trying to get my breath.

The desk sergeant was busy writing something in a blue hardbound notebook. He didn't even acknowledge me. I moved from one foot to the other, impatient for him to take notice of me, and urgently needing a wee.

He ignored me.

'Excuse me! I have a crime to report,' I said, a tremble in my voice.

As if he had all the time in the world, he put his pen down and looked up. 'A crime, you say. What would that be then? Lost your dog?'

I looked around. There were three young men watching me with interest. They sniggered. 'What sort of dog was it?' one of them asked, 'a poodle?' I gave him a death glare.

'I'd rather speak somewhere private,' I said to the officer, raising myself to my full five foot two inches, 'it's a matter of national security. Walls have ears.'

He lifted his eyebrows, 'Matter of national security, is it

now? Well, sit down over there, Missy, and I'll see if I can find someone to talk to you.'

I stayed right where I was, all the time checking the door in case Biggerstaff appeared.

'Before we do that, I'd better get your name to pass on to the detective.'

He closed the book he'd been writing in and took another from the shelf. He had dandruff on his shoulders and nails bitten down to the quick.

'Name?'

'Lily Baker, Private.'

'And what's the matter about?'

'I already said I'd rather discuss it somewhere private.'

He tutted, then turned his back on me, and picked up a phone on a desk behind him.

'Ted? Good. Girl here, ATS from the look of her, wants to talk to someone about a matter of national security.' A pause, 'no, she doesn't seem like a loony.' he listened for a minute, 'okay, thanks.'

'He says he'll be about ten minutes,' he waved a hand to where the lads sat, 'sit there. He'll come and get you when he's ready.'

Furious, I sat with my hands tucked under my arms, knee jiggling. The lads were talking about sport, laughing and teasing each other. A couple of times they tried to involve me in their conversation, but I was in no mood for small talk.

Twenty minutes later I stomped back to the desk.

'You said this Ted would be ten minutes. It's twenty now. This is an urgent matter.'

He looked at the clock on the wall, 'I expect he's got caught up in something. Give him a bit longer.'

I wanted to scream and stamp my foot like a two-year-old.

The door to the side of the desk opened and I jumped up, ready to tell this Ted what had happened. But it wasn't Ted, and it wasn't for me. A uniformed officer called the lads through and they vanished into the building with him.

Ten minutes later the door opened again, and an officer called my name.

'I'm Detective Sergeant Ted Wilson,' the officer said as we walked along the corridor. Painted a dull cream, it badly needed redecorating. It smelled of disinfectant and, faintly, of damp.

He stopped at a door on the left.

'Right, here we are. Come on in.'

It was a small square room, painted the same drab colour as the hall. There was no window. A rectangular table and two chairs were all bolted to the floor.

'Sit yourself down, Private. Now, you said you had a matter of national security to report. What's this matter that's so urgent? Is it going to ruin my afternoon?'

'It might do a lot worse than that,' I said, ignoring his sarcastic tone.

He leaned back in his chair and crossed his arms. 'Go on then, tell me your story. It'd better be a good one.'

My words came out in a hurried jumble, 'I work at the Deptford Army Depot and one of our suppliers is a Blackshirt. I saw him at a Blackshirt meeting just now. He should be arrested straight away. They all do.'

That made him unfold his arms. 'A Blackshirt you say. Have you got any evidence?'

'I just saw him in a meeting. I told you. A Blackshirt meeting. They had the big thunder-flash flag and everyone had Blackshirt armbands too.'

'Really? You're not making this up to get a bit of attention, are you? I know what you girls are like. And who is this 'him' you're talking about?'

I narrowed my eyes. 'I don't make things up. I sneaked in a back garden and saw Mr Biggerstaff...'

'Biggerstaff?' he interrupted, 'Is that John Biggerstaff? He's a very respected businessman. He does a lot for charity and contributes to the Police Widows Fund.'

'I don't know about that. But he supplies guns to our Depot and a lot of them go wrong. I think he sabotages them. I think he wants to stop Britain winning the war.'

He folded his arms again, 'That's a very grave accusation against someone of impeccable character.'

'Mr Biggerstaff is a supplier for Deptford Army Depot. A while ago he asked me to do some things for him. He offered to pay me.'

Wilson frowned, 'So you're in league with him?'

'Of course not. I'd hardly be here now if I was, would I?'

'Okay, he asked you to do some dodgy things. Did you do them?'

I sat back and folded my arms, 'The first thing I did was tell my boss, Mr McDonald, because I was suspicious of Biggerstaff.'

'Mr Biggerstaff, you mean.'

'If you like. My boss told me to go along with him and see what he was up to. All I ever did was deliver a little package. I don't know what was in it.'

'Okay, so far, so good. But how did you find out he was a Blackshirt?'

'I had an old newspaper. It was, well, it was in our WC and one day I noticed a picture of a Blackshirt march and he was in it.'

He laughed, 'So, an old paper from before Blackshirts were made illegal. That's hardly proof he's still one, is it. I don't believe he's involved in any such thing these days. Sounds to me like you're making this up.'

I wanted to punch him.

I stood up. 'Now, you listen to me. You're a public servant and I'm here volunteering information about national security. It's time you took what I was saying seriously. If not, I want to speak to your boss.'

Wilson gave an exaggerated sigh, 'Sit down for goodness' sake, and tell me the rest of this story.'

'Today I followed Biggerstaff...'

'Mr Biggerstaff.'

'Biggerstaff. I bumped into him and he said he was going to a meeting. He went to a house further down this street. The back gate was open, so I went in the garden and peered through the window.'

'So let me get this straight. You trespassed in someone's back garden. That's a criminal offence.'

I scowled at him, 'Don't be so silly.'

'Are you calling a police officer silly? You think I'm silly, do you?'

Heat flushed through my body, 'No, I didn't mean that. I'm here of my own free will to report a crime and you seem to be obstructive.'

He started to speak, but I held up my hand to stop him, 'I saw Biggerstaff and a load of other men in the Blackshirt meeting. He spotted me looking through the window and one of his goons chased me across the park behind the house. I got away.'

'You got away. What did you do, bite him in the knee?'

I stood up abruptly. 'I want to speak to your senior officer. I've had enough of this nonsense.'

He stood up too. 'Miss Baker, I've had enough of this nonsense too. You're under arrest for trespassing. You do not have to say anything, but anything you do say will be taken down and may be given in evidence.'

I couldn't believe what I was hearing. 'You're arresting ME? I came here to report a crime, you can't arrest ME.'

He shrugged. 'Actually, I can. I'm a police officer, it's what we do. And before I saw you, Mr Biggerstaff phoned me to warn me you're a trouble maker. A fantasist, he called you. Out to get him because he wouldn't go out with you.'

I laughed, 'Go out with him? You're joking. I wouldn't go out with him if he was the last man on earth. I want a solicitor. Now!'

He shrugged again, 'I expect you do. All in good time.'

He opened the door and stepped into the corridor. A minute later he came back with a policewoman.

'This is WPC Lake. She's going to take you to the cells.'

I spluttered, 'This is crazy! I'm here to report a crime! You can't lock me up!'

He turned to the policewoman, 'Take her to the cells. We'll leave her there until I decide what to do with her.'

I was so agitated I gabbled my story all over again to WPC Lake as we walked to the cells. She never said a word.

She opened the cell door and showed me in as if she was inviting me into her living room. It was about seven feet by ten with a semi-circular window high on the wall. The window had bars, and hanging from two of them were handcuffs. There was a metal frame bed with a thin mattress and a rough woollen blanket. Next to it was a hard-back chair and a metal stand with a wash-bowl in it. In the wash-bowl was a tin mug, a water jug and a small threadbare towel. The floor was concrete, and the walls were the same drab cream. It was hard to imagine a more depressing room.

'You're really going to lock me up?' I asked, 'I came here to report a crime. I'm not a criminal.'

She was tall for a woman and had brown curly hair. Her face was kind, but wearing a professional look. 'I'm afraid I don't make any decisions about that sort of thing. But I can make you a cup of tea or get you a glass of water.'

I plonked myself down on the excuse for a bed, 'I'll have tea, please.'

Fifteen minutes later she was back with the tea in a tin mug.

'Mr Biggerstaff, did you say?' she asked out of the blue.

'Yes. He's a Blackshirt and I think he's sabotaging guns he supplies to our Depot.'

She nodded but didn't respond.

'I'll check on you in about half an hour,' she said, and locked me in again.

The cell got colder, and I wrapped myself in the scratchy grey blanket. Outside I heard the dull rumble of traffic, and inside I heard people in other cells. All men by the sound of it. They shouted swear words and banged their tin mugs again and again demanding to be let out. I moved myself into the corner of the bed against the wall, and tried to block out the noise and the smell of wee.

Daylight faded and a weak light came on in the high ceiling. I had nothing to do but think. Was it possible that Wilson was in this with Biggerstaff, or did he believe what Biggerstaff said was true? If he was in it with him, it suggested the Blackshirt movement was wider than anyone knew. Were other police officers in on it? How high did it go?

A million questions whirled round it my mind, but the most pressing one was if I would be released. When I was,

Biggerstaff was going to be after me. Now he knew I knew about him, he wasn't going to let me go free. And with the police believing him rather than me, I couldn't work out what would happen. I'd tell Mr McDonald and he would go to the police - that was the best option. His position would surely carry more weight than mine, and he could insist on speaking to a senior officer. But if they let me out overnight, I'd have to go home. I wouldn't be able to see Mr McDonald until next day. Was it possible Biggerstaff knew where I lived? He could kill me before I even got to see my boss. I shivered at the thought. He had goons who worked for him. Would he order one of them to kill me? I rocked back and forward on the bed, my hands jammed under my armpits.

On her next check, the policewoman called through the grill, 'Do you want a sandwich?'

I sat up, 'Yes, and I need to go to the toilet,' I'd been waiting ages.

'There's a bucket in the corner for that.'

I looked at her in disbelief. 'You're kidding!'

'No, sorry! I'll come back with the sandwich.'

The fish-paste sandwich was dried, bread curling at the edges, but I ate it anyway to stop my stomach rumbling.

Half an hour later WPC Lake came back to collect the tin plate and mug. 'I'm off duty in a while, so someone else will be checking on you. Good luck!'

And with that she closed the grill, and I was alone again.

CHAPTER 26

*B*efore the next half-hour check was due, the door suddenly opened. A portly policeman stood there, a neutral look on his face.

'You're free to go,' he said.

I blinked. 'What? Free to go? Will I be charged?'

He shrugged his shoulders, 'I haven't been told anything about that. You can go. Have you got all your stuff?'

I grabbed my bag and gas mask and headed for the door, unable to believe this was happening. The policeman escorted me to the front desk without another word.

'Sign here, name and date,' he said, and thrust a red book under my nose.

'Right, off you go, and we don't want to see you again,' he said, then turned back and went through the internal door without another look.

I stood for a minute bemused, unsure what to do next. Then I decided to go back to the Depot, because I knew my way home from there.

But that wasn't to be.

With eyes closed, I took a deep breath of the cool night air outside the station. I raised my face to the light drizzle that prickled and tingled on my eyelids and felt my tension release. Another deep breath and I looked down the blacked-out street, and I stopped to orientate myself and decide on which direction to go. Going down the station steps into the darkness, I sensed, rather than heard, a presence behind me. I stopped breathing, fear rooting me to the spot. So near to the sanctuary of the Police Station, I briefly thought to step back into this small pool of light. But before I could move or even think further, an arm closed round my neck, and my arm was twisted up behind me.

A man's voice hissed in my ear, 'You're coming with me,' he said, 'keep your mouth shut or it'll be worse for you.'

Even as I struggled for air, there was no mistaking the whiskey sodden breath - Biggerstaff.

My stomach knotted, and I had an urgent need to pee. I attempted to turn: to free my arm, tugging with all my strength, but he was bigger and stronger than me.

Believing my life depended on it, I attempted to shout for help, but his grip reduced my cries to a helpless muted gurgle.

'I said shut your bloody mouth!' Biggerstaff said, his voice strident.

With frightening speed, he dragged me across the road. I recalled the training I'd received in self-defence, and desperately racked my head for the moves I'd learned. But the pace and violence of the attack, and the overwhelming fear numbed my thoughts and muscles.

As we entered the confines of the bombed church, I felt hope ebb from me like a wave retreats from the beach.

'So this is how it ends,' I thought with sadness, but also a strange acceptance. I thought of the people I'd have liked to say 'goodbye' to, and felt a pang of grief for those who would grieve for me. I briefly recalled the time when I saw the police digging up the body of the dismembered woman in a church. Was that his idea? Was this to be my end, after all I'd been through?

Then a sudden urge to survive burst within me and I shouted for help again. The cry was cut short as he punched me in the mouth. 'Shut it!' he hissed. I felt wetness from my nose and blood dripped into my mouth.

Yanking my arm again, he dragged me towards the back of the church opposite farthest away from the road and help. We slipped and staggered on falling debris, but never enough for him to loosen his grip. My heart beat at record speeds, and my breath came in painful gulps. I tripped over a fallen stone and he pulled me back upright, almost dislocating my shoulder.

'I'm sick of you interfering with my business, you little bitch,' he said, clutching my arm so hard it was like torture. 'But you won't be sticking your nose in it much longer!'

There was a little light from the moon, but it came and went as clouds scudded over it. Eerie shadows moved here and there, seeming to follow us. Parts of the church were still upright; an arch in front of us and window shapes either side. There was no roof. Weeds grew between the rubble and rubbish on the ground, softening our footsteps.

'Right,' he said, 'this'll do.' The moonlight was enough for me to see we were next to a set of stairs leading down to the crypt.

'He's going to kill me and throw me down those stairs,' I thought, 'no-one would find me for years.'

Then two things happened at once.

An air-raid siren wailed.

I saw a dark shadow move towards us from the road.

The sound of the siren distracted him, and he slackened his grip on a my arm just a little.

It was enough.

Ignoring the pain, I suddenly squatted down, twisted and yanked my arm away from him. Then I jumped up so I was nearer his height.

With the side of my hand, I chopped his Adam's Apple.

He made a gargling noise and doubled over.

It was the brief reprieve I needed.

But I'd only got a few steps when a deafening bang made me jump. It was loud enough to hear over the siren. The ground near me jumped too.

'I've got a gun here,' he said, still bent over, his voice rasping, 'get over here, you cow. I don't want to drag you.'

I didn't move.

He fired another shot at my feet.

I moved a few inches nearer the steps.

A cloud moved away from the moon and I saw, behind him, the darker shape move. He hadn't spotted it yet.

I wasn't sure, but I thought it was WPC Lake, the police-woman who hardly said a word to me in the police station. Her footsteps were drowned by the sound of the siren and people in the street running to their shelters.

She was coming to help me!

I moved around so Biggerstaff's back was to my rescuer. But by now I was dangerously close to those crypt steps, and I felt sweat on my brow and upper lip.

The policewoman was a few steps closer when she tripped over and some masonry fell over. Biggerstaff spun round.

Swearing, he fired his gun at her. There was a loud bang and a flash of light.

His shot went wide.

She charged him head first and, simultaneously, I jumped on his back. Unbalanced, he fired again, but the bullet bounced harmlessly off some bricks.

With a roar, he reared up and shoved his arms back, pushing me backwards, then thrust the policewoman away. I righted myself and looked round for a weapon.

He stood looking from one of us to the other, then aimed his gun at me.

Without thinking, I threw the piece of masonry I'd picked up at his head, using all the force I could muster. It didn't hit him full on as I'd hoped, but hit his ear. He clutched it and swore loudly.

WPC Lake pulled out her truncheon and, her arm swinging wide, bought it down on his head.

He staggered, grasping his bleeding forehead, and then, arms windmilling, he fell backwards as if in slow motion.

Down the crypt steps.

Into the darkness.

For a second I stood without breathing. Was that it? Was the nightmare over?

'Is he unconscious?' I whispered, only then realising the siren had stopped.

'I don't know.' she said, 'be careful. He's still got the gun.'

Keeping to the side, she shone her torch down the steps. The gun lay three steps down, and Biggerstaff was at the bottom. Unmoving.

'Come on, let's check,' she said, her voice hushed, 'grab the gun in case he goes for us.'

Despite my army training, the weight and feel of the gun was alien in my trembling hand.

Side by side, we went down the stairs expecting Biggerstaff to leap up any moment and attack us.

When we got closer, it was obvious he was dead; his head was at an impossible angle and his blank eyes were open, unseeing, blind.

'What do we do?' I muttered, as much to myself as the policewoman.

She bent down and picked up my cap, 'Here, don't leave this behind. We did to him what he planned to do to you. We leave him there. Wipe your fingerprints off the gun and throw it down beside him. We're getting out of here fast!'

My heart beating fast, I had an overwhelming urge to run away from the church as fast as I could, but sense overtook panic and I forced myself to walk at a normal pace. I didn't want to attract attention to myself. *Take deep breaths, take deep breaths,* I told myself as I walked towards the bus stop. The streets were empty, most people being in the shelter, but as always, a few stragglers were heading who knows where. It was like I expected a big sign above my head saying *Murderer.*

I glanced in a window and saw what a mess I looked. My tie was crooked, one of my buttons was undone, and my hair had escaped from my cap. My fingers trembled so much it took three goes to do up the button, and my hair kept falling out of my cap as fast as I pushed it in.

When I looked respectable again, I continued on my way. My legs were slow, but my mind raced. He's dead, Biggerstaff is dead, we killed him. The words went over and over in my mind - running round like a rat on a wheel in a cage. A little voice nudged in, saying he was going to kill me, and WPC Lake hadn't intended to cause his death; but guilt shouted louder in my brain. I stood at the bus stop and tried to make myself change the words I said to myself, *He was going to kill you, you're not responsible.*

It didn't work, and I stood for ages guilt clutching my stomach.

Then the All Clear sounded and people began to come out of the shelters.

An elderly man joined me at the bus stop. His back was so bent he only saw the floor. He had to keep stopping to lift his head with his hand to see where he was going, poor man.

'Tell me when the number seventy two comes along will you Love?' he asked.

With a quiet groan, he eased himself onto the bench at the stop and chatted without pausing for breath. I had no idea what he was saying. He didn't seem to notice.

The bus stopped right next to us before I saw it, and the noise of people getting off dragged me away from my awful thoughts enough to help the man get on. During the whole journey my shoulders were as stiff as an unopened book. I even missed my bus stop and had to walk back from the next one.

My hands shaking, I turned the key in the front door, and heard the wireless on in living room. Bronwyn was home! I was so relieved I staggered against the wall.

'What's up with you, Sweetheart?' Bronwyn asked as I walked into the living room, 'you look like you've seen a ghost.'

I promptly started to cry.

She put her arm round my shoulders and guided me to a chair, 'Sit down there while I get you a drink of water.'

She was back in seconds, putting the glass in my hands. Then she sat next to me without speaking, waiting for me to calm down. My sobs gradually lessened until they became snivels. 'It's Biggerstaff...' I couldn't go on.

'What's he been up to this time?'

I told her the whole sorry story, breaking off several times to cry again or explain something she didn't understand from my garbled words.

When I'd finished, she sat back in her chair, 'So let me see if I've got this right. Biggerstaff arranged to have you arrested. Then he arranged for you to be released at a convenient time for him to kidnap and kill you. Is that the long and short of it?'

I blew my runny nose and wiped my wet cheeks, 'That's right, I... we...'

'So if he hadn't died... and you didn't kill him, by the way... he'd have killed you.'

I nodded. I knew that, of course, but hearing someone else say it really helped. That little voice in my head tried saying, *It wasn't my fault, it wasn't my fault.*

Bronwyn went into the kitchen again and came back with two bottles of beer. 'Here, I got these at the off-licence on the way home,' she took the tops off, 'go on, it'll put hair on your chest.'

I laughed, 'I don't need hair on my chest,' I said, 'I need a clear conscience.'

We sat in silence as we drank the beer straight from the bottle like the soldiers we were.

'I'm going to say something serious now,' Bronwyn said, 'if you heard the story you'd just told about someone else and not you, would you think they ought to feel guilty?'

I took another swig of beer. It wasn't very strong, but I felt the alcohol slow my whirling brain. I tried to imagine Bronwyn, or Edith, or Marion or Ruth telling me the story, and I realised she was right. I wouldn't have thought they had anything to feel guilty about.

Bronwyn finished her beer and put the bottle on the floor, 'Are you going to tell Mr McDonald? Didn't he ask you to report anything dodgy about Biggerstaff?'

I bit my lips, 'I haven't even thought about that, but it would be stupid to tell him. He doesn't need to know. The fewer people who know, the better.'

She patted my arm, 'Well, I won't tell a soul, your secret is safe with me. Anyway, he'll soon find another supplier for the Depot. That's all that's important to him.'

I wasn't sure if it was the beer or the tension, but I could hardly keep my eyes open. 'I'm going to have an early night, Bron. Thanks for being such a good pal.'

I fell asleep straight away, but my dreams were full of churches and truncheons and blood.

CHAPTER 27

A few days later we were leaving the office at the end of the day when the air-raid siren sounded. No matter how often I heard it, it still made me start and experience a tremor of dread.

'Oh, not again!' Ruth said, 'Just when I wanted to get home early. I hope my children are safe somewhere.' she buttoned up her jacket. 'Come on, girls, let's hurry to the shelter.'

Marion moved more slowly now her stomach was big enough to throw off her centre of balance. Several times Ruth had asked her if she was sure her dates were right, but Marion just shrugged, uncertain.

A light drizzle started as we hurried out of the building and the busy pavements were slick and shining. Marion, who was walking beside me, slipped on some wet leaves and almost fell. I grabbed her and pulled her upright, but she yelped and held her stomach, teeth clenched tight.

'Are you okay? Can you make it?' I asked anxiously.

'I'll be all right,' she said, although she wasn't convincing.

The nearest shelter was a road away, only a couple of hundred yards at most, yet it seemed like a mile. ARP wardens were directing people; helping the elderly and lame, and encouraging the dawdlers who were so busy looking for planes that they got in the way.

As we neared the shelter people rushed past us wanting to get in quickly, and we were jostled and pushed from all sides. Like everyone else, I'd had to hurry to shelters before, and the siren did its job of inducing that sense of urgency, panic.

I put my arm around Marion to protect her, and Bronwyn got the other side. To our alarm, Marion kept doubling over, gritting her teeth with obvious pain. Bronwyn looked at me and raised an eyebrow. Her meaning was obvious - is Marion in labour? I shrugged my shoulders, unsure. It was too early by the date she said, but she'd never been certain of it.

We were feet away from the shelter when the rain came down in force; big farthing size drops splashing on the pavements, soaking us in seconds. Those still outside pulled coats over their heads, or put up umbrellas which slowed entry as they stopped to put them down.

The shelter was a little less crowded than usual at first, perhaps because many people were still at work or enjoying an early evening film. We stood inside the door, but were soon pushed along by others coming in just as wet as we were. Soon the floor was soaking and a draught from the door made me shiver.

Marion was standing, but bent over, groaning and holding her back.

'Can someone give Marion a space, please?' I asked the nearest group and they squashed up along the wooden bench seat and made space for her.

I whispered to Bronwyn, 'Have you ever delivered a baby?'

'No,' she whispered back, 'but I've had the training. Have you?'

I nodded. I'd been trained in childbirth too, but never needed to use it. 'With any luck this is a false alarm,' I said.

I squatted down in front of Marion, 'How are you now? Any more pains?'

She said no, then seconds later clutched herself and doubled over again. Edith, who'd been watching all this closely, wriggled in next to her. 'Is it happening?' she asked, 'hold my hand, squeeze as tight as you like.'

I used my watch to time from that contraction. To my dismay, the next one came five minutes later. She needed to be in hospital, and fast.

'You're lucky, Ducks,' a woman near her said, 'you're going to 'ave this one quick. I was in labour thirty-two hours with my first and the others weren't much better.'

'An' me,' another one said, 'twenty-five hours; thought the little bleeder would never come out.'

I bent down again, 'Marion, I'm going outside to ask the ARP warden to get an ambulance.'

She nodded and tried to smile.

'I'll look after her,' Edith said, 'and Ruth and Bronwyn are here too.'

'And I've delivered two nippers down our road,' the nearby woman said, 'nothing to it. We'll make sure you're all right.'

I struggled past all the others who were sitting on the benches or, in some cases, lying under them. 'EMERGENCY!' I shouted twice when people were slow to move, 'LET ME THROUGH!'

'Stand back,' I said to a couple near the door, 'I have to go outside.'

'You're not supposed to, it's against the rules!' a pin-thin woman said in a very bossy voice. She was wearing her wrap-around pinny and bedroom slippers.

Opening the door as little as possible to avoid light spilling out, I slid out sideways, knocking my hat off and scraping my ear. I needn't have bothered because it wasn't dark yet, but it's hard to let go of habits sometimes.

The warden I knew was still out there. 'I need an ambulance, Mark,' I said, 'my friend's in labour in there.'

'Crikey,' he said, taking off his tin hat and scratching his head, 'Can you go to a phone box, Love? There's only me on duty here just now, and I daren't leave. You know what it's like.'

The Depot office was all locked up by then, so it meant running to the nearest phone box. That was in the opposite direction.

The rain had eased off to a drizzle, but I was glad I'd retrieved my hat to keep my head dry.

The streets were mostly empty although, as always happened, there were a few people here and there scurrying toward the shelter late. When that first happened and I was on ARP duties I felt irritated with them. They were taking risks with their lives. Then someone I worked with explained they might have been in the middle of something they couldn't stop immediately. Perhaps helping an old person or having some medical treatment. I was put to shame, and resolved to be more forgiving in the future.

The anti-aircraft guns were firing, their criss-cross lights illuminating the sky and the barrage balloons. As always, the combination of the siren, the bullets whizzing through the air and fear of death, made my adrenaline high.

By the time I reached the phone box I was out of breath and had a stitch in my side, but glad to see it was empty. One window was broken, and it reeked of wee, but it was in working order for once. I reached into my purse and took out some pennies. I knew the number by heart from calling it many times on duty. I picked up the handset and dialled, then put the money in the slot and pressed Button A to connect.

'Quick, I need an ambulance, someone's in labour in the in the Amhurst Street shelter.' I shouted, trying to be heard above the siren.

'What? Who is this?'

I put my mouth to the phone and cupped my hand round it. 'I SAID,' I spoke slowly, 'I need an ambulance, someone is in labour in the shelter in Amhurst Street.'

'Who's calling please?' the very patient voice on the other end said. She'd raised her voice too.

'It's Lily Baker, I'm an ARP warden but I'm not on duty at the moment. It's my friend Marion who's in labour. How long will the ambulance be?'

'Wait a minute, caller.'

I put another coin in the box while I waited and automatically checked the little tray under Button B. That was the button to press for reject or unused coins. As children we all checked them in case we were lucky enough to find a coin left behind. My friend even used to stuff a bit of material up inside on the way to school and pull it out on the way back. 'Some daft sods think the machine's gone wrong and kept their money, then they give up,' he used to say, 'more for me!'

'Caller? Are you there?' the voice said after a short delay, 'We've instructed the ambulance team, but I've just been told a building has collapsed on their route so they will take longer than they normally would. Is the birth imminent?'

'I'm not sure, but I don't think it'll be long.' My stomach turned over at the thought of it.

'If you're ARP, you've presumably had childbirth training. Is there anything you need to know before you go?'

'No thanks, I'd better get back.'

As I ran back I reviewed my training. Wash hands, towels, what else was it? My mind was blank. Surely, between me and Bronwyn and all the experienced ladies, we'd manage. As long as everything went straightforward.

Then a bomb fell a few streets away, and without thinking I dropped to the ground and put my hands over my head. The sound of the explosion echoed as it reverberated round the streets, joined by terrifying crashes as buildings fell. My first instinct was to go into Air Raid Warden mode and run round there to help. Then I thought better of it - Marion needed me. Picking myself up, I ran the rest of the way, almost tripping over several times as I dodged potholes and pieces of debris. When I got back I hammered on the door to be let in. The same officious woman was standing just inside, her arms folded.

She tutted, 'That's twice you've put us in danger by making us open the door. Haven't you ever heard of the blackout?'

'Oh, do shut up, you stupid woman, it's not even dark yet!' I said, and brushed past her. I knew I'd feel guilty about my outburst later, but was too irritated to worry about it.

I found my little group. They'd cleared a lot of people off the narrow seat, and Marion was lying down clutching her stomach, her face screwed up tight in pain.

I looked at Bronwyn and she put her mouth to my ear, 'It won't be long, It's going to happen soon. Is the ambulance coming?'

'Not soon enough,' I said, 'roads blocked.'

The woman who said she'd delivered babies stood up and came to us. 'Right, you girls, let's get organised. Get a few people to form a ring round her, backs to her. Give the poor girl some privacy.'

While we followed her instructions, she shouted, 'Who's got a clean hanky or towel or anything?'

People nearby began searching through pockets and bags, but she didn't have much luck; only six clean hankies. She turned her back to the room and bent forward a little, then wriggled out of her petticoat. 'That'll help,' she said, 'make do and mend and all that.'

She checked the cordon was in place, then leaned over and spoke to Marion.

'Right Marion, my girl, let's see what's going on here. I'm Doris, and I know what I'm doing. Nothing to worry about. Open your legs. This is no time for modesty.'

Marion groaned, and Doris watched her closely, 'She'd been pushing for a while now. It's not going to be long.'

It was only then we realised Marion's waters had broken and her skirt and knickers were soaking.

Marion sobbed, 'I've wet myself,' she cried.

'No, you haven't. This is what happens when you're about to have your little one. Now, open your legs like I said. Don't worry, I've seen it all before!'

She pulled down Marion's wet knickers, but kept her skirt over her raised knees.

'Got a torch?' she asked me.

Being shielded, my torch wasn't very bright but it would have to do. She bent down and shone it close to Marion's privates, having a good look. Then she straightened up and spoke to her,

'You're only going to need a few more pushes, Love. You're the lucky one. You'll soon be cuddling your baby. Now, hold your friend's hand tight and push as hard as you can when you need to.'

The people near enough to overhear the conversation were silent, apart from the odd word of encouragement.

Edith was still kneeling on the floor holding Marion's hand, 'Give it all you can, Marion, not long now.'

Four more pushes and Doris said, 'There, the head's out now. One more push and you'll be cuddling your little one.'

I saw her put her hands either side of the baby's head, 'This one's got plenty of hair,' she said with a smile, 'just like my Tommy.'

It was no time before we heard the baby cry. I looked down, and it was unbelievably tiny.

'It's a girl!' Doris said, and began wiping her clean with one of the hankies, 'she's a little one, but she's got a good pair of lungs on her. She'll be okay.'

There was a round of applause, and shouts of congratulations from people nearby. It lifted our spirits after the tension of the delivery.

Doris wrapped the baby in her own petticoat and laid her on Marion's chest. Marion put her arms around her newborn, looked down at her and burst into tears.

'What's all this, then?' Doris said, 'did you want a boy?'

'It's not that,' Marion said, 'it's… it's…'

'Well, you've still got to give one big push, young lady, and get that afterbirth out.'

Marion was beginning to push when the door burst open and the ambulance crew rushed in. They took one look at the situation and told us to stand aside.

'Leave it to us,' they said, 'you've done a great job, Missus. Have a sit-down and let us do the rest.'

Bronwyn and I had tears of joy running down our cheeks, and Edith was crying as much as Marion.

'Our baby,' she said, stroking the baby's head.

CHAPTER 28

The trees in the square opposite our flat were finally giving up their late summer finery. Flame-red leaves twisted and danced in the breeze unwilling to reach the ground. It had rained earlier, and the long afternoon shadows threw patterns on the shiny pavements. A couple from a few doors along walked past, dressed up for an evening out. She wore a white fitted jacket with a black flared skirt, high heels and a big black hat with a white ribbon round it.

'Not kidding nor nothing, but that outfit must have cost more than we earn in a month,' Bronwyn said, 'Wonder if we'll ever be able to afford nice clothes like hers?'

'We'll have to get promotion or find a rich man for that.'

After a warm few days, the temperature was cooler and I pulled my coat closer as we walked to the bus stop.

'What did you say this policewoman's name was?' Bronwyn asked as we dodged sandbags and kids whizzing past on their scooters.

'Susan. Susan Lake. I owe her my life.' I thought back to the awful night, not long before, when Biggerstaff tried to kill me. He'd probably have succeeded if she hadn't come along.

'It was kind of her to write, and I'm really looking forward to seeing her again.'

I had a bar of chocolate in my bag; the biggest possible with my rationing. I hoped she liked chocolate, but reasoned that everyone did.

'Hey,' Bronwyn said, 'I had a letter from Wendy who used to live upstairs. It came today. Really it was for both of us. She's staying with her sister and she sounds as if she's doing okay. Never even mentioned her good-for-nothing husband. She's applied to train as a nurse with the Queen Alexander's. Good for her.'

'I hope she meets a man who'll love her like she deserves,' I said, 'I never understood why she stayed with that awful husband of hers.'

Bronwyn gave a bitter laugh, 'You know nothing, Girl. Lots of women stay with rotters. My mum never had the money to leave: it was like being in prison. Your mum must have been the same.'

I nodded, 'You're not kidding, but Susan wasn't that broke and her sister would have let her stay.'

She linked her arm through mine, 'Do you remember that film Gaslight? The one where the husband convinces his wife she's going crazy? Well, some men play mind games like that and the women think they can't manage without them. I remember one woman who lived near us in Swansea. Her old man was the pits, he kept her short of money, called her all the pigging names under the sun and beat her black and blue. She thought it was all her fault, 'cos he convinced her it was, the louse. When he died we cheered and thought she'd be happy, but at the funeral when they lowered the coffin into the ground she tried to throw herself in with him. Screaming and crying something rotten she was. The vicar had to hold her back! You couldn't make it up.'

After a ten minute wait the bus came and it was so crowded we had to stand for the twenty minute journey swaying this way and that as we went round corners. The bus was full of women with bags of shopping on their laps, and men in flat caps who looked like they'd just finished work at a nearby armaments factory. Peering between other passengers, I spotted an ARP man warden on a church roof using binoculars to search the sky for bombers. I hoped he wouldn't find any.

The Crown and Feathers was about a mile from the police station where Susan worked. It was a square building on the corner of two roads with three long windows either side of the door and three more round the side. The street was full of people hurrying to or from work and a man on a veg stall outside was trying to tempt shoppers with muddy potatoes and insect-ridden cauliflowers. Even though vegetables weren't rationed, he had plenty of customers.

We were early so we went in to wait for Susan. The pub had well-worn patterned carpets and red imitation velvet curtains. Red, white and blue bunting hung over the bar looking patriotic, and a picture of the King was on one wall. The barman wore a white cotton coat and a big white apron over the top, stretched round his lavish stomach. He looked more like a butcher than a barman.

Half a dozen men in overalls were propping up the bar, drinking pints and chatting about their boss.

'Bloody Idiot!'

'He almost got me killed!'

'I'd like to kill him!'

One of them turned and noticed us, 'Can we get you one, Girls?' he asked, 'Girls shouldn't have to go to the bar, that's men's work.'

'Honest to God, it's like being in Swansea sometimes.

They don't serve women at the bar there. You can stand there all night. They pretend not to see you.'

But she said it quietly so he couldn't hear her, and smiled sweetly when he asked again what we wanted.

'Let him pay. Serve him right for being so daft,' she said as we found ourselves a corner table a long way from them. We sat back, put our bags and gas masks down and took a swig of our drinks. 'I wonder if any of them ever did anything as dangerous as we did when we were in France.'

'Let's hope all the things women have done so far in this war will make men like him realise we're not all silly girls without a brain in our heads.'

'Silly girls fit for nothing but being a housewife and mother,' she said pulling a face.

The door opened and we looked up, but it was an elderly couple dragging a wicker shopping basket on wheels. The man wore a grey coat and a trilby hat and the woman had a faded blue coat with a matching knitted bobble hat. He helped her sit down and then went to the bar.

'Have you heard the news about Marion's baby?' I asked Bronwyn.

'About Edith adopting it? It's the best news I've heard all year. Her and Sidney want a family and she says he's okay around children. Do you know when Marion will give her up?'

'They've decided six weeks. It must be so awful for Marion, but she can feed her and they can look after her between them. They decided to call her Patricia. The nice thing is Marion can keep in touch. She's going to pretend to just be a friend of the family.'

Bronwyn tapped her fingers on the table, 'That's good, but it'll be tough on her. I don't know what I'd prefer, never seeing my baby or seeing it often but having to pretend not to be who you are. What if you didn't like the way the new parents were bringing your baby up? It'd be just awful because you wouldn't be able to do anything about it.

'It reminds me of a family that lived near us. We all thought Mrs French was the little boy's mother, but it turned out she was his grandmother. The lad was bought up to think his actual mum was his aunt. She lived with them too. She was only fifteen when she had him; just a nipper herself. At least they didn't throw her out like Marion's dad would have done. Where's Marion going to live anyway? Is she going back to her mum and dad's?'

I wiped the shandy from my mouth. 'She says she's not. She'll be able to go back to work so she wants to rent a room somewhere. Says she doesn't want to ever see her dad again.'

Bronwyn gave a low whistle. 'Never! Poor kid. She'll have a tough time affording rooms on her own on what she gets paid.'

'It's going to break her heart giving up her baby, that's for sure. And that stinker of a boyfriend of hers just carries on his life like nothing happened. I hope his wife gives him hell every day.'

The elderly man came back from the bar with two ciders, kissed his wife on the cheek and sat next to her holding her hand.

'That's the sort of relationship I want,' I said.

Bronwyn looked over at them, a sad smile on her face. 'Never had any like that in my family. Anyway, how're you feeling about Edward these days, Cariad? Did you do the right thing breaking up with him?'

I tested my feelings. I'd believed Edward and I would grow old together like the elderly couple in the pub, but too much time, distance and too many experiences put paid to that.

'I'm feeling okay, it was the right thing to do even though it was sad. Did I tell you he'd got someone else in mind? He'd been waiting to see if we had really finished before he asked her out. I hope they'll be happy together, he deserves that. He's a good man.'

'Have you ever thought about that evening when you all went to Vanessa's?'

I nodded, 'Yes, what about it?'

'If you think back to what you were all told, it's all come true. Wendy was told she'd have awful news and it would be the best thing that ever happened to her…'

I saw where she was going, 'and her rotten husband died.'

'Marion was told she'd have great sadness, but more to look forward to.'

I pulled a face, 'We don't know if she'll get that bit yet.'

'No, but at least she'll see her baby and she's young yet. And, of course, your nan told you you'd be in danger. She certainly wasn't wrong there!'

The door opening interrupted us and this time it was Susan. She looked quite different out of her police uniform and I almost didn't recognise her. She'd been in uniform when we had that awful incident with Biggerstaff and we didn't stay together very long after we realised he was dead. We'd quickly discussed our cover story in case we needed it, then swapped addresses and went our separate ways.

I got up and hugged her, smelling her flowery perfume. 'I'm so glad you came, Susan. Let me get you a drink. What will you have?'

'Can I have a gin and tonic?' she asked, and took off her dark blue coat and hat.

'Let me get it so you two can chat,' Bronwyn said, getting out of her seat.

'I don't know how I can ever thank you enough for saving

me the other night,' I said, 'without you I probably wouldn't be here.'

She laughed, 'I don't know, you were doing pretty well chopping him in the neck even if you did have to jump up to do it!'

'Hey, I can't help being short!'

Bronwyn came back in no time, 'Come on then, you two, tell me all about it.'

I sipped some more of my lager, 'I've told you all about what happened when I got home, Bron.'

She looked around and lowered her voice, 'But did you really just leave the... him... where he was? Weren't you worried someone might have seen you?'

I looked at Susan to answer. She leaned forward and spoke just as quietly, 'Yes, we left him. We were lucky no-one saw us, but we were well back in the ruined church away from the road.'

My heart jumped, 'Have they found him yet?'

She nodded, 'Yes, a couple of days ago. He must have been getting a bit whiffy because a dog smelled him and ran down the stairs. Its owner reported it. Must have been a bad start to his day, poor man.'

'Bloody hell!' Bronwyn said.

I hated Biggerstaff but the thought of him lying there for days, gradually rotting, twisted my stomach. If only there had been some other way to deal with him. I put my hand over Susan's. 'Do they realise what happened?'

She gave a little grin, 'That's the best thing. They think it was some sort of criminal gang killing. Apparently he was well known for being in with some dodgy people...'

'Blackshirts.' I said, interrupting her.

'That's right, but criminals too, not just traitors. So that's what they're investigating and we're off the hook! Serves him bloody well right. I think the honest cops are glad he's dead and won't waste too much time trying to find his killer.'

'But what I don't understand,' Bronwyn said, 'is why you were outside the police station when Lily was released. Was that just a coincidence?'

The elderly couple finished their ciders and stood up, straightening their backs with a groan. We stopped talking until they'd gone.

The door closed with a creak, 'Lily didn't stop gabbling as I took her to the cells. I never said anything to her, but I knew there was something dodgy going on and I'd heard about you-know-who. I think he was pally with the officer who interviewed Lily. That would explain why they arrested her when she hadn't done anything wrong.'

'So that's why you waited outside?'

The door creaked open again and two men came in. We waited until they'd gone to the bar where the chat was enough to cover our conversation.

'I waited outside because I heard them saying what time Lily would be released and I was due to go off duty about then. I never for a minute thought she'd be grabbed by you-know-who. He must have told whoever he was paying when to let her go so he could be ready to drag her off.' She looked around again, 'All I was going to do was tell her not to trust any of the officers in our station because I had no idea how many of them were in you-know-who's pay.'

Bronwyn sat back in her chair, 'Well I never. So, it's just good luck that she's lived to tell the tale. But I've got to ask you, do you feel guilty about it? What happened to you-know-who?' she asked looking from one of us to the other.

'I've thought about that a lot and the truth is, I don't. You helped me with that,' I wondered how best to explain it, 'he was trying to kill me, that's for sure and he was supplying sabotaged guns and boots to hinder the war effort. And in the end it was an accident that he died.'

Susan leaned forward again, her voice a whisper. 'That's right, I was trying to protect Lily, not kill him. In my books that means we can sleep easy at night.'

Bronwyn raised her glass, 'Here's to the two of you. Two brave women who rid the world of a dangerous man.'

I lifted my glass too. 'That's right, and we've got a new friend,' I said, then I dug in my bag and handed Susan the chocolate. 'A bar of chocolate isn't much in return for what you did but I hope we'll keep in touch and I'll have more chances to repay you.'

She broke the chocolate in three, 'Come on, Girls, let's share this!'

Lily Baker Series:

The Picture House Girls

The Telephone Girls

The ARP Girls

Standalone Books:

Winner Takes All

Murder, mystery and Magic˙

Non Fiction:

How to be Assertive

Time Management for the Office

The Assertive Social Worker

The EI Advantage (with Susan Maitland)

CVs and Applications

Excel at Interviews

Study Skills for Success

ACKNOWLEDGMENTS

As always I would like to thank the many people who helped me with this book. My husband Rick for helping me with plot ideas, my friend Fran Johnston (Smith) for ideas and masses of general support, and Maggie Scott for brilliant proof-reading.

Thanks also to my kind readers who offered opinions, spotted any last typos and were invaluable:

- Dreena Collins
- Margaret Smith
- Samantha Sherratt
- Jacqui Kemp

Printed in Great Britain
by Amazon